NELL OF GUMBLING

My Extremely Normal Fairy-Tale Life

EMMA STEINKELLNER

LABYRINTH ROAD | NEW YORK

The Magical and Fairyful Tales of Gumbling

Text copyright © 2023 by Emma Steinkellner

Cover art and interior illustrations copyright © 2023 by Emma Steinkellner

All rights reserved. Published in the United States by Labyrinth Road, an imprint of Random House Children's Books, a division of Penguin Random House LLC, New York.

Labyrinth Road and the colophon are trademarks of Penguin Random House LLC.

RH Graphic with the book design is a trademark of Penguin Random House LLC.

Visit us on the Web! rhcbooks.com

Educators and librarians, for a variety of teaching tools, visit us at RHTeachersLibrarians.com

Library of Congress Cataloging-in-Publication Data is available upon request.

ISBN 978-0-593-57066-1 (hardcover) — ISBN 978-0-593-57069-2 (paperback) — ISBN 978-0-593-57067-8 (lib. bdg.) — ISBN 978-0-593-57068-5 (ebook)

The text of this book is set in 14-point Nell Handwriting.

Interior design by Juliet Goodman

MANUFACTURED IN CHINA

10 9 8 7 6 5 4 3 2 1

First Edition

FOR TEAM STEINKELLNER:
I love this family of ours.

Dear Journal,
My name is Nell and I'm twelve. The first pages of all my journals are like that:

This one had a velvety cover and a lock and key, but I lost the key. See ya!

My name is Nell and I'm eleven. mermaid

My name is NELL and I'm ten. Draw 1 square. Draw another square. Draw lines to connect corners. Now it's 3D!

My name is Pavlova and I'm nine.

When I was nine, I tried to get everyone to start calling me Pavlova,* but it didn't stick.

Then a few pages into every journal, I give up. It's not my fault—it just gets really boring! BUT . . . this time, I will keep this journal. I have to. If I'm going to take myself seriously as a writer and an artist, I need to make a commitment to my craft.

This is what Dad calls a "high-stakes situation," and I have to rise to the challenge.

* Note:
A pavlova is a dessert named after a famous ballerina.

← FRUIT
← CREAM
← MERINGUE

ANNA PAVLOVA

She wore flowers under her hair. (How'd she make them stay?)

So, like I said, I'm Nell (short for Lenore) Starkeeper, and I'm twelve. This is me (see below).

THE THREE WAYS I WEAR MY HAIR:

1. TWO BRAIDS DOWN
Makes me look the most like a little kid, so I don't do it a lot anymore.

2. TWO BRAIDS ON TOP
My favorite because it makes me feel like an old-fashioned lady who has one of those sticks with two buckets

LA LA♪ LAAA!

3. ALL THE WAY DOWN
Keeps my neck warm, but I have so much hair that it gets in my mouth when I talk. Ew.

Big nose, big glasses, big ears. They all fit on my head, though.

4 plunks 7 peeples tall (That's 4 feet, 9 inches or almost 1.5 meters.)

THINGS I ALWAYS HAVE WITH ME:

my journal (from now on)

pencils, pens, and coloring stuff

Bruise-y, scrape-y scabby arms and legs from climbing trees and walking backward

a travel-size charging star (Pa makes me take it everywhere for emergencies, because I'm the oldest kid so I have to be responsible.)

Okay, I should clear up some stuff. Dad grew up way, way far away, and he says he never heard of plunks, peeples, or charging stars till he moved here. So, if any of this sounds strange, I'll explain "here" a little more . . .

GUMBLING

Formerly known as "the Most Precious Kingdom of Gumbling"
(I live here.)

It's not a kingdom now because 100-ish years ago, the king of Gumbling
stepped down from the throne (he didn't think there should be a king
anymore). And then he disappeared. So now it's just "Gumbling."

Hills

Gumbling River

Wild Hoofbeast
Reserve

Valley

Lifty
Thing

**Starkeeper
Star Farm**
My house and my family's farm.
I can go into more detail
about it later.

Workshop

Thumblestump
My second-best friend and
neighbor, Gilligan Bugg, is a
Thumbkin, so his whole family
lives comfortably in the tree
stump next to my house.

Forest

Yabulga's Hut
This is where Yabulga
the Witch lives. We try to
avoid it. She really hates
when anyone gets
near her house.

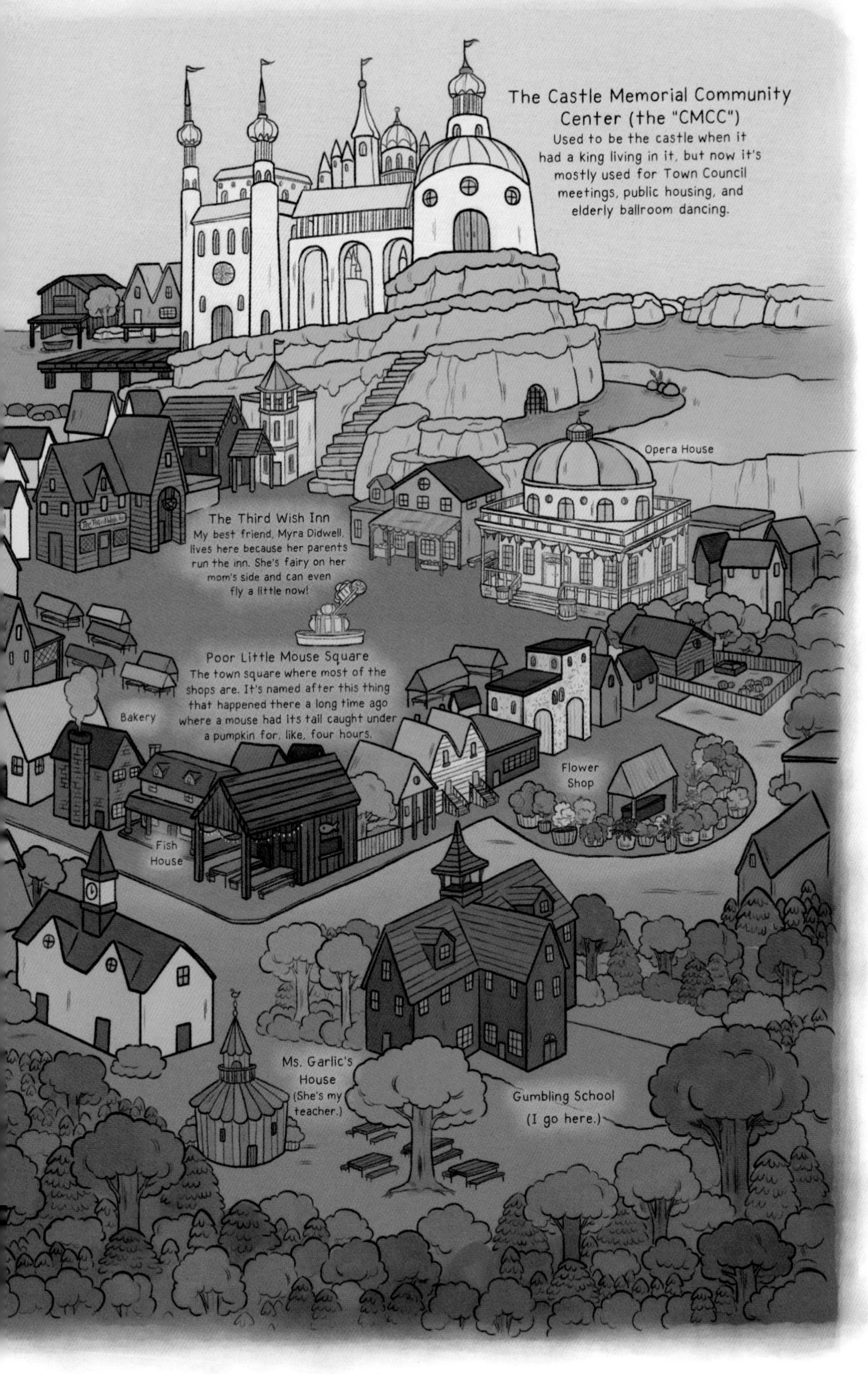

The Castle Memorial Community Center (the "CMCC")
Used to be the castle when it had a king living in it, but now it's mostly used for Town Council meetings, public housing, and elderly ballroom dancing.
Opera House
The Third Wish Inn
My best friend, Myra Didwell, lives here because her parents run the inn. She's fairy on her mom's side and can even fly a little now!
Poor Little Mouse Square
The town square where most of the shops are. It's named after this thing that happened there a long time ago where a mouse had its tail caught under a pumpkin for, like, four hours.
Bakery
Flower Shop
Fish House
Ms. Garlic's House (She's my teacher.)
Gumbling School (I go here.)

Out-of-towners think living in Gumbling is like some kind of fairy tale, like Cinderella or Sleeping Beauty or something. It really isn't, it's just... I don't know, regular! Like, I have friends and go to school just like any kid. SPEAKING of school, tomorrow we get our...

Tomorrow is the day that all the seventh graders at Gumbling School get assigned our apprenticeships. We will "learn the tools of a trade from a real working person in town" by working with them after school for three months.

Why is this the most important, most significant, most game-changing day of my life? Because I know, I just KNOW, I'm going to be assigned to apprentice with the town's most famous artist...

Wiz Bravo

He's amazing. Not only has he been chosen to paint the ceiling fresco of the Gumbling Opera House and half the paintings at the museum, but he's also a big deal even outside of Gumbling. He's showcased art in Paris, Tokyo, New York... I want to be him.

Maybe someday when I'm a famous Wiz Bravo-type artiste, this journal will be in a museum, too. And people can see what my life was like when I was a kid. If you're a museum person in the future, this is for you:

MY HOUSE

(Drawing my house like this gave me a headache.)

I live in the top room now. I used to share with Schmitty, but my dads said if I cleaned out the attic, I could make it my new room. It's definitely an adjustment, but now I have some PRIVACY so I can work in PEACE.

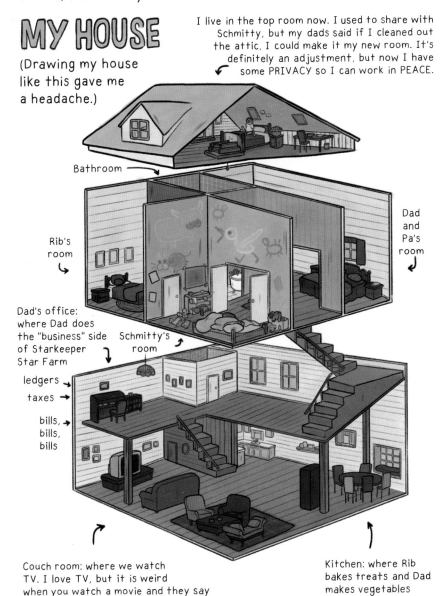

Bathroom

Rib's room

Dad and Pa's room

Dad's office: where Dad does the "business" side of Starkeeper Star Farm

Schmitty's room

ledgers

taxes

bills, bills, bills

Couch room: where we watch TV. I love TV, but it is weird when you watch a movie and they say magic isn't real! Well, maybe not for them, but haven't those dips ever heard of Gumbling???

Kitchen: where Rib bakes treats and Dad makes vegetables

And here's... # STARKEEPER STAR FARM.

All around the world, people can't touch the stars because they're too far away and too hot. Not in Gumbling! The King Star Fairy gave a patch of stars to the poor Starkeeper family a long, long time ago to help them. That's why the stars hang so low in Gumbling Valley and why we can touch them without getting burnt to a crisp. No big deal, right?

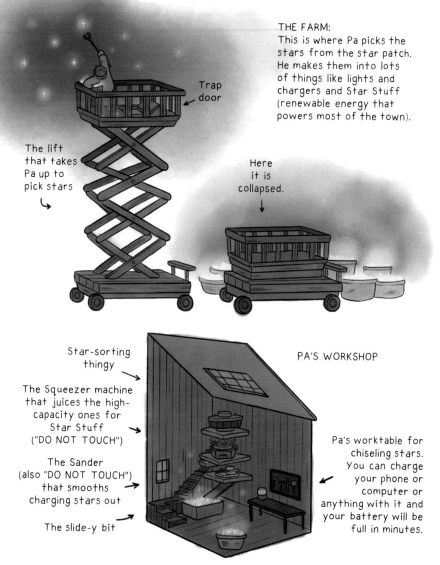

Trap door

THE FARM:
This is where Pa picks the stars from the star patch. He makes them into lots of things like lights and chargers and Star Stuff (renewable energy that powers most of the town).

The lift that takes Pa up to pick stars ↳

Here it is collapsed. ↓

Star-sorting thingy →

The Squeezer machine that juices the high-capacity ones for Star Stuff ("DO NOT TOUCH") →

The Sander (also "DO NOT TOUCH") that smooths charging stars out →

The slide-y bit →

PA'S WORKSHOP

Pa's worktable for chiseling stars. You can charge your phone or computer or anything with it and your battery will be full in minutes.

MY FAMILY

PA

WHAT HE'S LIKE

Really fun and silly and jolly

HE LIKES TO

Hum and sing while he works

LA LA LA LA

HE'S GOOD AT

Laughing. His laugh is the loudest laugh I've ever heard, and he loves to laugh.

HA! HA!

LOVES

His big red beard. He says he's had it since he was sixteen years old!

SMELLS LIKE

His old chore coat that he wears when he works. It smells like stars. (If you've never smelled stars before, they smell a little like burnt popcorn.)

DAD

WHAT HE'S LIKE

Nice, but strict. He doesn't laugh as much as Pa, but when he does, it's really cool.

LOVES

The big calendar in the kitchen and soft, wrinkle-free sweaters

SEPTEMBER

Dad's iron

sss!

SMELLS LIKE

Plain soap

HE'S GOOD AT

Having good ideas. It was his idea for me to wear the braids on top of my head so I wouldn't eat my hair anymore.

7

My little brother, **RIB**

(short for "Ribwort")

WHAT HE'S LIKE

He's only ten, but he takes care of everybody, making treats and cleaning up all the time.

SOME TREATS RIB MAKES

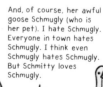

HE'S GOOD AT

Baking/cooking. And he just checked out a book on junior spellcraft from the library, so he's trying out magic. He'll probably be perfect at it.

SMELLS LIKE

Cookies

LOVES

Dad says Rib has a "tender heart" because he loves everybody and wants to make life nice for the people he loves.

My baby sister, **SCHMITTY**

(short for "Schmideline")

WHAT SHE'S LIKE

She's six, and she's a LOT. Dad and Pa call her "an active little girl"— I call her a mess. Which they say isn't nice, but they didn't have to share a room with her!

SHE'S GOOD AT

Playing and having fun and burping and spilling and tracking mud. She's so funny.

LOVES

Bumping my elbow when I'm trying to draw or write

See?!
Told you!

HER ANIMAL FRIENDS INCLUDE

Lovely Lana the milk snail

Crook the talking gumblebug (who she has taught five words to)

SMELLS LIKE

Her animal friends

Big Girl the wild Hoofbeast

And, of course, her awful goose Schmugly (who is her pet). I hate Schmugly. Everyone in town hates Schmugly. I think even Schmugly hates Schmugly. But Schmitty loves Schmugly.

So, that's my life, future museum people. Normal-ish, huh? But when I am selected as Wiz Bravo's apprentice, it'll all change forever. And I'm one hundred percent absolutely, positively sure I'll get picked because my teacher, Ms. Garlic, had us rank our top three choices for our mentor and hand them in. And here's a copy of mine:

Nell S.

RANK YOUR TOP 3 APPRENTICESHIP MENTOR CHOICES
(You might not get your first choice, but you will have an enriching apprenticeship experience no matter what!)

1. WIZ BRAVO, ARTIST
2. WIZ BRAVO, ARTIST
3. WIZ BRAVO, ARTIST!!!

This is a little strategy on my part.

Much like Schmitty blocking all the doors and windows so Schmugly can't fly away, I am corralling Ms. Garlic—guiding her. I leave her with no option but to pair me with Wiz Bravo so I may start on my path to destiny and one day become an incredible writer and artist.

Me now:

nobody special

Me later:

famous artist, beloved by all

I discussed my scheme with the family at dinner.

This was new. I'm used to getting the lecture from Dad and a ton of praise from Pa. Now all of a sudden they're switching things up? A little consistency would be nice!

VERY helpful as always, Schmugly. I love my family a lot, and I care what they think. But I also care what I think, which is this: I'm not a child anymore, and I can't just waffle on who I want to be or have unrealistic goals like being a goose. I will be a great artist, and this apprenticeship is my best shot.

Dear Journal,

In approximately twenty minutes, I will receive my apprenticeship
assignment and begin learning from the legendary Wiz Bravo.
I am as nervous as a baby Hoofbeast before its first stampede.
I'm sitting in the auditorium with Myra and Gilligan.

MYRA

ME

GIL

Myra got honey on her wing at breakfast, and Gil is sitting on
my shoulder and watching me draw. He says he likes the way I
exaggerate things when I draw, making them a little funnier,
like cartoons.

BEST FRIENDS!

11

Their top three apprenticeship mentor choices were:

1. Rosasol Luna
the Town
Council Member

2. Harbert Link
the Public Works Director

3. Principal Pfluff
the School Principal

Myra is a planner, an organizer, and generally a go-getter.
She wants to make things happen, so it makes sense that all
her picks are all leadership-y. I would let her tell me what to
do forever—she's very good at it.

1. Mr. Grubbisher
the Garbage Collector

2. Mr. and Mrs. Didwell
the Innkeepers

3. Koji Font
the Printer

Gil's picks are a little random. He said he'd be interested in
doing pretty much anything. He's extremely chill like that.

He's also outrageously
handsome and brilliant, something like a god.

Gil wrote this.

Voila Lala just trotted up to me and, TOTALLY UNPROMPTED, snorted that Wiz Bravo would never let me be his apprentice because my drawings aren't realistic enough.

NOT REALISTIC ENOUGH???! She's so stuck-up just because her mom, Bahbra Lala, is the star at the opera house, and she knows she can get her apprenticeship there. Blegh. Well, here is a VERY realistic portrait of Voila Lala:

Horn that she always sticks in everybody's business

Glowing red eyes that look for mean little things to point out

Sharp, pointy teeth

MORE "REALISTIC" VERSION OF VOILA

Clompy, stompy hooves

Still not very realistic, darling.

Note: Okay, this may or may not be totally realistic (her eyes and teeth aren't red or pointy). I'm venting. But who cares?? That's art, isn't it? She doesn't get it.

Anyway, I have to go now! They're about to make the announcements!! See you when I'm Wiz Bravo's apprentice!!!! Aaaahhhh!!!

"Sadness"

A Poem by Nell Starkeeper

Life is pain.

Life is ice cream melting in your hand.
Cold.
Sticky.
Not creamy.
Not sweet.

Life is a Hoofbeast that tramples your heart
And crumples your dreams.
Life is a paper cut, how it stings, how it burns.
Life bites your tongue. It stubs your toe.

Life paints you a picture of exactly what you want
And frames it so clearly for you to see.
Every detail in place
A perfect
Realistic
Work of art

Then

When you least expect it

Life takes it all away from you.

Because Life is just mean like that.

Dear Journal,

I didn't get it. My life is ruined.

Dad tried to give me a pep talk, but I couldn't hear it.

Pa gave me what I'm sure was a really good hug, but I was too numb to feel it.

Rib made me spot bread, and it turned to ash in my mouth.

Schmitty shoved Schmugly in my face and made him nuzzle me, which was THE WORST.

I will not be apprenticing with Wiz Bravo. No. That little dream flew away, like Gilligan that time it was windy and he forgot to wear his weighted vest.

Who, you may ask, will be the next great artist of Gumbling?

Leabelle Oh.

Leabelle Oh. And why not? On top of being super pretty and really nice and liked by everybody, she is a really great artist. Better than great. Amazing. Better than amazing. Realistic. She knows how to do shading and perspective and all that advanced stuff!

Sometimes when I see what she's painting in art class, I don't even wanna try anymore.

At the town art fair, she got first prize. I got "Participant."

And don't get me started on when we both made Ms. Garlic birthday cards.

That's very nice, Nell.

Oh my word, this is STUNNING!

And I am dirt. Ugh, Voila was right. Wiz Bravo selected the best artist in the school, and it wasn't even a difficult choice.

And I haven't even gotten to the worst part: my actual apprenticeship assignment. I have to apprentice with Mrs. Birdneck, the Town Lorekeeper. It's terrible. Here is a list of everything that makes it terrible.

9 REASONS WHY I GOT THE WORST APPRENTICESHIP

1. I have to spend my whole apprenticeship watching Mrs. Birdneck sort unbelievably boring town lore, documents and articles that I don't care about.

2. Mrs. Birdneck is weird and old and shush-y. One time, Myra and Gilligan and I were in the park joking around and she shushed us! At the park! Who does that???

3. Myra's older sister apprenticed with Mrs. Birdneck when she was in seventh grade, and she says Birdneck always evaluates her apprentices really harshly and they almost never get a good grade.

4. Mrs. Birdneck's office is in the Town Archives at the CMCC. Which will be dusty. And musty. And covered in cobwebs. My allergies will be on fire.

5. I will be wasting all this time after school doing something I will hate instead of drawing and improving as an artist.

6. I'll be "Nell Starkeeper the Lorekeeper," which sounds too matchy-matchy.

7. Basically everyone else got their first choice! Myra's going to learn how to be a council member. Gilligan's going to be collecting garbage. Leabelle will be painting gorgeous artworks with Wiz Bravo.

8. At the end of my apprenticeship, I have to give a presentation on everything I learned (which will be nothing) in front of the whole school.

9. Just BECAUSE!

I have emerged from my room—and my head is a little clearer. Dad and Rib are watching a movie in the Couch Room about this girl who has to work at a fashion magazine, even though she really doesn't want to, and her mean boss is monologuing at her about the color blue.

I see my future. Only my boss will be telling me about the joys of shushing. And the only fashion will be the special gloves I have to wear to prevent my finger oils from getting on the precious archival material.

I don't think I even have finger oils! That sounds more like Schmitty. Who, by the way, is spinning in circles trying to make herself dizzy right now.

Pa was in his workshop. I asked him if what he said before, about not wanting to work on the star farm when he was a kid, was true. And if it was, when did he start liking it?

Things aren't always under our control. But that means we get to be surprised by the good things that come our way.

It just doesn't feel like a good surprise. It feels like I got stuck with this because I'm bad at art.

Now, who said you're bad at art?

A kid at school said my art wasn't "realistic."

Aw, Nell.

Then he said,

I think your drawings have a lot of realism to them. You capture things the way you see them and create a world that's vibrant and interesting and funny and unmistakably made by you. No one can take that away from you.

But if you can get a new perspective and try to see things in a new way, you can really grow as an artist.

I tried thinking about that. But then I just started to feel sick to my stomach thinking about tomorrow.

Dear Journal,

Okay. It's a new day. It's the first day of my apprenticeship, and I need to at least start with a good attitude. I read what I wrote yesterday, and I sound so bratty. I don't want to be That Nell. I want to be the Nell my dads think I can be.

I've got school till three, then just ninety measly minutes with Mrs. Birdneck. I can do it.

I picked up Gilligan from the Thumblestump on my way to school. Which means I literally picked him up. He tried to hold back how excited he was for his first day doing garbage collection with Mr. Grubbisher. I told him it's okay, I don't mind.

Mom said I have to wear my reflective vest, just in case I fall in the garbage. I told her, Mom, calm down, I'm not gonna fall in the garbage.

I think I can be a real asset to Mr. Grubbisher. Maybe I can look out for really small pieces of trash!

By the time we got to Myra's, she was already outside waiting (very Myra of her). She was "dressed for success" and had her game face on.

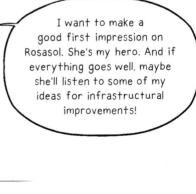

I want to make a good first impression on Rosasol. She's my hero. And if everything goes well, maybe she'll listen to some of my ideas for infrastructural improvements!

This school day seemed to go by weirdly fast. Ms. Garlic had us fill out a survey about our apprenticeship assignments, but I didn't know how honest to be. I don't want her to think I'm mad at her for assigning me to Mrs. Birdneck. I don't even know if I am. I just don't know why she did it. To punish me? Was it just random?

I just did this:

Nell S.

APPRENTICESHIP ASSIGNMENT SURVEY

How satisfied are you with your apprenticeship assignment?

How much do you feel you have to learn from your mentor?

VERY LITTLE   A LITTLE BIT   (QUITE A LOT)   VERY MUCH

Any questions?

How did you pick our mentors?

Myra and me both have our apprenticeships at the Castle Memorial Community Center, so we walked there together. Well, I walked, and she switched between walking and flying.

Gotta get my reps in!

On our way up the hill, we saw a man and a lady taking pictures of the castle. They looked a little too sharply dressed to be tourists, and most out-of-towners stay at the Third Wish anyway, so Myra definitely would have recognized them.

At the front desk, a Thumbkin receptionist gave us directions. He told Myra to take a left to the main hallway and second door on the right for Rosasol Luna's office.

Then he asked me where I was going.

Mrs. Birdneck's office. The Town Archives?

So . . . you'll hang a right and go down the big, winding staircase till you hit . . . the dungeon.

The dungeon?

Well, it's just a funny nickname. It's not a dungeon anymore. It just . . . used to be.

It's getting harder to stay positive here.

As I climbed down the long, endless, not-entirely-structurally-sound spiral staircase, I began to feel sick again. Just like last night.

Then, finally, I was at the bottom. The unfriendly-looking door was marked "Earla Birdneck, Town Lorekeeper," so—unfortunately—I was in the right place.

I opened the door a crack.

Okay . . . I closed the door.

Almost a minute later, Mrs. Birdneck opened the door again. She was like a lady in a portrait in a haunted house.

I looked behind me. It was as dark as night in the entryway, so I wasn't sure what light she was worried about.

"Well. Come in, then."

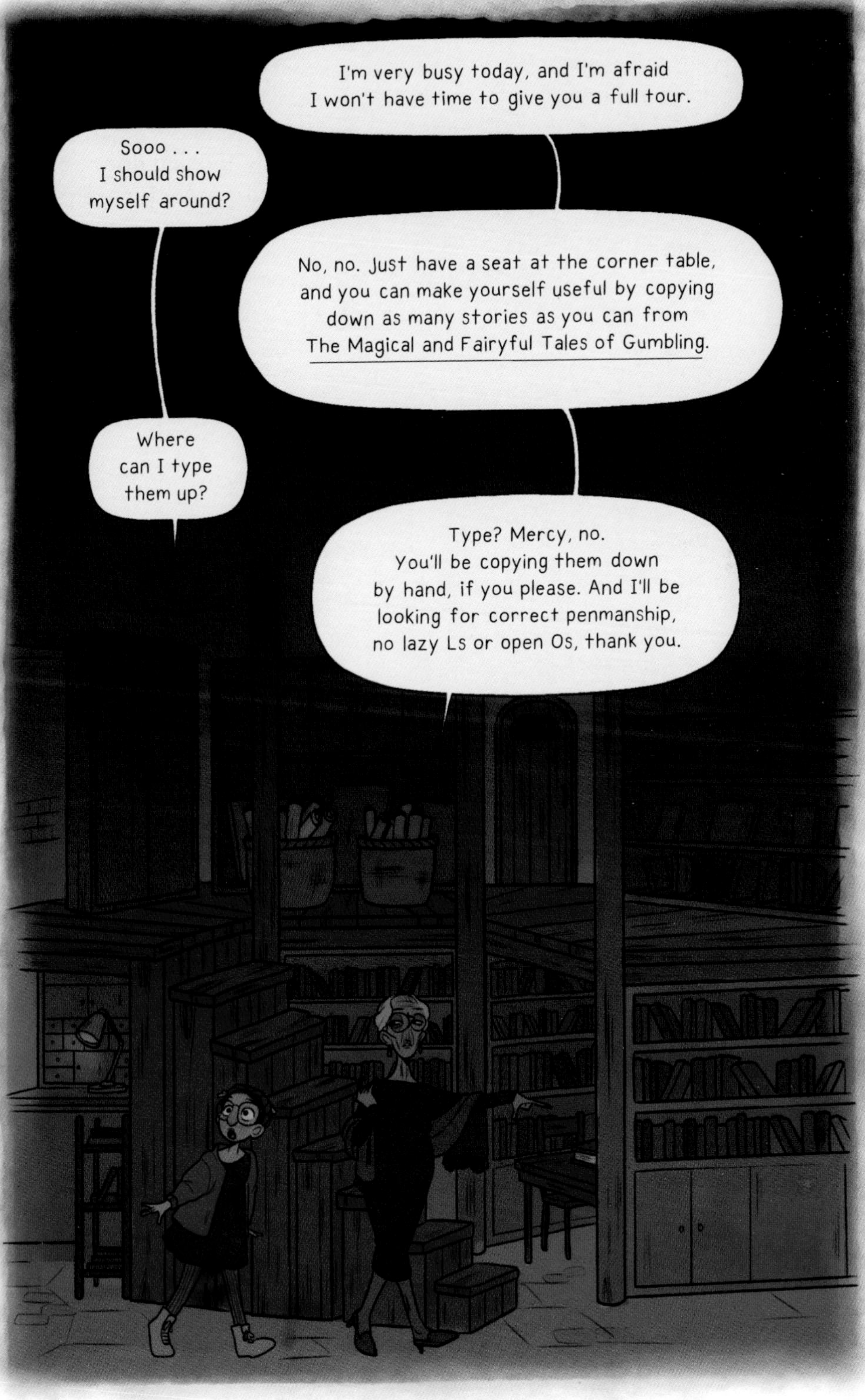
I'm very busy today, and I'm afraid I won't have time to give you a full tour.
Sooo . . . I should show myself around?
No, no. Just have a seat at the corner table, and you can make yourself useful by copying down as many stories as you can from The Magical and Fairyful Tales of Gumbling.
Where can I type them up?
Type? Mercy, no. You'll be copying them down by hand, if you please. And I'll be looking for correct penmanship, no lazy Ls or open Os, thank you.

Lucky me. I get to develop a debilitating wrist condition copying down stories for babies. I'm copying down one of the stories in here so I can remember how uniquely, soul-suckingly boring this day was. Enjoy! (And remember, penmanship counts! 😑)

How Gumbling Came to Be

The part of the world where Gumbling is now was once home to a family of giants.

They ate trees and splashed in the puddle that to us is our big and crystal-clear lake. The giants loved to romp around and play, but the baby giant was a softhearted thing. Not one for rowdy games and rough sport, she often needed time to herself. So one fine day, she settled herself in a warm spot in the sun. And she found it so pleasant that she returned the next day. And day after day after that, she returned. Until it became the custom every day to go there and sit, to read giant books or draw giant pictures or think giant thoughts.

And by and by, the surrounding creatures came to agree that it was a very nice place to be. And animals, who were tiny to her, would come rest there, too. Hoofbeasts that were to her like caterpillars are to us grazed the waving grasses.

The first person to come along was Yabulga. She built her hut deep in the forest where her magic moss could grow the best. The baby giant would say hello every day, and Yabulga would grunt. Then more people came along, family by family. There was so much in that land to support the newcomers. Good sunlight and rain and plants and dirt.

And the baby giant felt good that they liked it there, but she missed that time alone. So away she went to find another spot to sit. And, being very thankful for the gift, the people named the town "Gumbling," which is what the giant said her name was. But she was, after all, only a baby so she might have been babbling.

I copied down seven stories before five o' clock. When I told Mrs. Birdneck I had to go, she looked at all of them and snorted and said she'd see me tomorrow.

I walked up the staircase and looked back at the door. It didn't look like she'd be going home anytime soon. Is this what she does every day? How does she stand it? She must like it, but WHY?

Those weren't even the good Gumbling stories, not like the one Pa told me about the first Starkeepers in Gumbling.

His ancestors were poor farmers, struggling during Gumbling's coldest, longest winter. They wished and wished and prayed for something that would save them. Then the King Star Fairy, Centaurus, said if they cleared a field, he would send down a patch of stars to Gumbling Valley for them to pick so they could have warmth and light that would last them through the winter.

That's a story! Not just some randoms building a town in the impression of a big baby butt.

I think this is the beginning of a loooooong apprenticeship.

Dear Journal,

Myra and Gil and me met at the Third Wish after we finished our apprenticeships so we could talk all about them. We took our regular booth right by the kitchen door where we can see Myra's dad cook.

We always share a bowl of blowtorch soup. It's really, REALLY, really good.

The Third Wish

SOUPS

Our Famous Blowtorch Soup
Tomato soup with a crackly, brûléed cheese lid, served with hot fries. We recommend dipping!

Dinghy Putt
Traditional Gumbling fish stew with spicy, robust shellibles, thumbfish, and dumplings

Garlic's Cream of Pepper
The Garlic family's own recipe! Roasted garlic and peppers blended with cream and butter

SANDWICHES

The Wamboom
Grilled Hoofbeast cheese and underberry jelly on sourdough

Classic Roust Roll
Battered and fried river-caught roust on a roll

The Opera House
Olive butter and smoked peppers on rye

Myra's Favorite Breakfast Sandwich
Scrambled goose eggs, cheese, and fairy greens on a biscuit

SPECIALTIES

The Lighthouse
Blackened roust with hand-swirled gravy and biscuits

The Third Wish Bowl
A split goose egg on hot pepper noodles with cheese and vinegar

The Disappearing King
(only on Fridays)
Roasted Gumblehawk and dumplings on a bed of mushrooms, served with pickled cabbage

TREATS

Gumquat Jelly and Custard

Underberry Pie

Flamed Lullipeach and Custard

Frozen Boiled Ice Cream
(served with fresh-baked spot bread)

DRINKS

Water

Hoofbeast Milk

Fizzes
(apple, gumquat, or lullipeach)

Or choose from a selection of Mrs. Didwell's traditional fairy teas

Hot Chocolate

Lemonade

Gil got up on the rim of the bowl AGAIN even though he's not supposed to. He always jokes that he's gonna jump on the cheese and crack it.

Well, today he actually did it. And he—of course—fell right in.

Gil's riding high on his first day collecting garbage with Mr. Grubbisher. I don't think I've ever seen him this happy.

I'm really, really happy for Gil and Myra. It seems like they're really inspired by their mentors. And their mentors really like having them around. I guess I just envy them.

Mrs. Snort-Snort Birdneck clearly doesn't even want me there. And it's not like I WANT to be there anyway, but if she thought I were cool and helpful, I'd feel a little better.

It's the people we saw taking all those photos of the castle. Tourists, maybe?

WET NAILS

She takes pictures of everything. Unless she wants to be in the picture—then he takes it.

They look a little alike, not twins, but maybe brother and sister.

TEETH

He has the biggest, whitest, teethiest teeth I've ever seen.

He has those phone things in his ears. The ones that make you look like you're talking to yourself if you're making a phone call (which he always is).

Her nails looked all glossy and wet. Like every time she snaps, some water's gonna flick off.

We eavesdropped on them a little. (I know it's a bad habit, but sometimes it's too hard not to.)

They saw us looking. Then they talked quieter, and we could only hear a couple words.

Then they got up and left.

Poor Myra. When your parents run an inn, there are always strangers sleeping in your house. Like, Rib's a little wiener and sometimes he's so nice it's annoying, and Schmitty is always sticky and gross, but I'd rather live with them than with some snobby strangers.

It's not like I hate out-of-towners. They're mostly all right. During the summer when there are more tourists, Pa and Dad even run a tour of the star farm, and we meet a lot of interesting people and make some extra money. That's kind of fun.

So it's not like some creepy movie about a weirdo village that's like, "We don't take kindly to outsiders," and then they use travelers as a blood sacrifice. (Although that would be a cool movie. We don't watch scary movies at my house because Rib's too chicken and Dad says we have to pick movies that work for everybody.)

Anyway, most out-of-towners are fine. But we get some sometimes who just treat us like we're souvenirs. They take pictures of us and our stuff and they don't even ask. One time a rowdy guy picked up Gil's mom and joked around like he was going to throw her. They can get impatient and rude and disrespectful. It's a huge bummer.

I don't know, maybe it's because they expect something different? I mean, I've seen movies about magic, and Dad's told me about how he had to adjust his expectations when he moved here. When people think about a place like Gumbling, they think fairies and witches and castles. They probably think they're going on a trip to some mystical other world.

And then when they get here, they're bored, because . . . well, we're a little bit boring. Fairies have jobs, and our town witch doesn't want to talk to anyone, and our castle hasn't had any princesses in it for decades.

They want it to be like this.

I dropped Gil off at the Thumblestump, and I was heading inside when I heard this strange clip-clop-clip-clop noise coming from the other side of our porch.

It was Voila Lala. At my house. Great.

Um. What are you doing here?

This is my house. What are you doing here?

Oh. "Starkeeper Farms." Duh. Of course it's your house. I have to do my apprenticeship here, with your dad. The farmer one.

Fantastic. Voila is going to be at my house every day. Life just keeps handing me fun little treats.

Making conversation with Voila is kind of a nightmare.
She always has something negative to say. I'm like that, too,
sometimes. But I try not to be.

But I'm sure dear Maman can speak to Ms. Garlic about this little faux pas.

Then I can get reassigned to a job that's more my style, and I won't have to see you and you won't have to see me.

FINE. BY. ME!

Actually, I'm pretty sure I got the apprenticeship no one wanted.

Oh yes, you're with what's-her-face, that scary library lady.

Guess what? It's not in a library. It's in a DUNGEON.

Ew. Ew ew ew. Please don't tell me any more about your sad life.

Voila's mom's assistant came to pick her up in this little bejeweled wagon. I tried not to laugh, but I giggled a little.

Don't laugh! New shoes really hurt, and it doesn't help that I've been doing farm chores all afternoon.

I didn't say anything.

Hmph.

It is a little funny, Voila.

Then they rolled away. Boy, is Voila a piece of work.

I guess we have something in common, though. Neither of us exactly got our dream apprenticeship. I'm stuck in the dungeon, and she's doing manual labor for the first time ever.

Of course, it's probably good to not always get what you want. Helps you grow and become a better person. But it's hard to actually feel yourself growing in real time. And it's very easy to feel the other part—being disappointed and wishing things were different. I'm feeling it hard-core.

"Voila got picked up."

"She's a character, huh?"

"Tell me about it. So . . . she's your apprentice?"

"Yep. I don't think star farming is her idea of a good time yet. Then again, it wasn't mine, either, back in the day. I hadn't found the fun in it yet."

""Found the fun"?"

"Yeah. It took a while for me to notice the things I'd come to love about star farming."

"Like how small Gumbling looks when I'm way up high in my lift. I feel like a giant. Or the big calm that washes over me when I'm in my workshop, chiseling charging stars. That little "tink-tink-tink" sound is very relaxing."

Pa said some people find the fun in the sight, smell, or sound of what they're doing. Or the outlook on life it gives them. Some people like the funny, interesting surprises. Some people like the satisfaction of getting it all done. There has to be something I can like in lorekeeping. I just have to try harder.

Dear Journal,
When Gil and I went to get Myra for school, we saw Wet Nails and Teeth again. But this time, they actually talked to us.

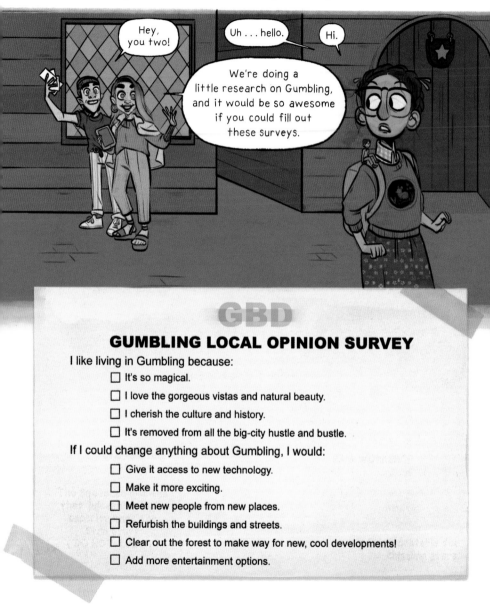

It's kind of a funny survey to take about the place you live. I don't think of Gumbling in that way. It's just home to me.

When we got to Ms. Garlic's room, everyone was bunched up in the corner. We couldn't see what they were crowding around, so Myra flew up to the ceiling to get a better look.

That makes sense. She started working for a celebrity, so she's kind of a celebrity now, too.

When Leabelle walked by, I swear she smelled like success. Or strawberry yogurt. Voila looked pretty ticked off. (Her mom and Ms. Garlic decided it would be good for her to keep apprenticing with Pa, in a character-building way.)

In art class, we used watercolors (my favorite) to make trees.
This is how you do it:

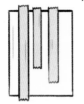 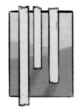 

1. Put down masking tape anywhere you want to stay blank.

2. Paint all around the tape.

3. Let the paint dry.

4. Lift up the tape, and then you can paint more or use pens for little details.

Myra and I taped a bunch of paintings together and stuck them around a big jar. Then Gil walked in place while we turned the paper circle around. It made it look like he was walking in a watercolor forest!

That's so amazing!

Leabelle sat down to watch. Gil tripped over his feet. He has a huge crush on Leabelle. (In case it wasn't super clear, a lot of kids have huge crushes on Leabelle.)

To be totally honest, it made me feel really self-conscious. She's so good at everything, and when she looks at what I've made, I can't relax. Even when she says something nice.

Then she turned to me.

Nell, can I ask you an art question?

Oh! Um . . . sure.

So I'm helping Mr. Bravo do a big painting in the opera house lobby. And I'm having a hard time getting it.

My brain is telling me Voila probably told Leabelle I wanted the Wiz Bravo apprenticeship. So now Leabelle's trying to be nice by making the apprenticeship sound like it's not that great. But I have to tell my BRAIN to stop thinking and actually listen to her.

See, usually when I'm drawing, it's just of one thing. But this painting is of lots of scenes in one story. Like a comic. And I thought, "Nell knows a lot about comics." I don't even know what I'm asking for. I just feel kind of lost.

I . . . have some comics in my backpack if you want to borrow them?

You mean it? Thank you so much, Nell!

I gave her some of my better comics. Peach-Pit Puckett!, Mosswall Mysteries, and The Knucklehead Brothers.

I'll be careful not to crumple them.

Don't worry about it.

Good friends make disappointment easier to take. They'll try to get you to feel better and help you have fun. But it's probably hard to be a friend when something good happens to you and not to your friend. I'm afraid Myra and Gil feel like they have to do all this extra work so I'll feel better. But I don't know how to tell them I don't need that.

Why is talking to your friends the simplest thing in the world sometimes, and then other times, there's nothing more confusing?

Dear Journal,

Sorry it's been a little bit since the last time I wrote in you. I've been kind of busy. With what, you ask? A few things:

Homework. We just have a lot lately. We had to do animal reports, and I chose to do mine on geese. I figured it would be easy because I live with one, but my research taught me that Schmugly is kind of bad at being a goose.

For example, geese usually travel in big groups. (A group of geese is actually called a gaggle.) Schmugly doesn't have any goose friends. Also, ~~gooses~~ geese (I keep doing that!) are monogamous, which means they mate with one other goose for life. And if Schmugly doesn't have any goose friends, you can bet he doesn't have a goose love life.

Now, when I talked about my report at dinner, Schmitty started crying! She took it all personally and thought I was being mean about Schmugly. I wasn't! I was just stating the facts. Dad made me apologize to her. (I did, but I didn't really mean it. I mean, how can you really mean an apology when you don't even know what you're supposed to be apologizing for?)

I got an A-minus on my goose report, which is really good for me.

WHAT???

Math quizzes. Now, those are a different story. We're starting to get into algebra, and it's not pretty. I look at all the letters and numbers smashed together, and I feel my brain float out of my body and fly away. She says, "Good luck, Nell, but I'm out." Dad's been helping me study, but we both get pretty frustrated.

I've also been really busy because after school, I help Dad and Pa get ready for the Holiday Feszht. That's still a couple weeks away now. It's the big winter holiday festival in Gumbling.

The town has done the Feszht for . . . I don't know. A long, long time. Everyone sets up these stalls in the town square, and they have food and hot drinks and gifts and stuff. There's music and dancing and games, and it's a lot of fun. But one of the most important parts of the celebration is the lights, which my dads are in charge of.

You would think Pa wouldn't need my help, since he already has an apprentice. But I guess Voila is pretty checked out when she comes to work at the farm. Pa says she's on her phone a lot, which doesn't surprise me. I think she scares Pa even more than she scares me, so he never asks her to do better.

So I have to help. Pa and Dad and I detangle lights as we watch a movie every night. It's actually really fun. I shouldn't complain about it.

And, of course, I still have to go to my apprenticeship every day after school.

No, it hasn't gotten better. If anything, it's gotten worse. Way worse. I don't even have the energy to write in this journal when I get home because I spend all stupid afternoon copying down stupid stories that nobody cares about at all. I'm SO over it.

Oh, but don't worry. When she's not making me copy down sentences like some thirteenth-century monk, there's plenty of other fascinating chores I can do. Such as:

Vacuuming every corner of the dungeon (not that it matters, because as soon as I'm done, new dust settles in immediately)

Rotating new books and documents into the "display" section (not that it matters, because no one, and I mean NO ONE, comes down to see that place)

Pasting and patching up the oldest bits of parchment (which also happen to be the worst-smelling bits of parchment—and the paste doesn't smell amazing, either)

And let's just say Birdneck and I aren't the best of friends. At least on my first day, she was busy enough that she left me alone. But now that I'm doing more tasks, she's always all up in my business, telling me what I'm doing wrong. Nothing is ever good enough for her, I swear.

Either my handwriting is too sloppy or I misspelled something or I missed a spot vacuuming or I'm vacuuming too loudly (?!) or I pulled out the wrong copy of A Traveler's Guide to Gumbling ("I asked for the edition from Winter 1935, NOT Midwinter 1935!") or, heaven forbid, I let one teeny-tiny drop of paste drip onto her precious, dusty stone dungeon floor!

Not to mention, she's always picking on me for stuff that isn't even part of the job! Like, she gets on my case for fidgeting or humming. I yawned the other day, and she said I would catch a spider in my mouth if I didn't watch my behavior. What is this lady's deal? Like she's never yawned!

And I haven't even told you her least favorite thing about me: my scabby knees.

Today she really got under my skin. She got me started on filing under the "Birdneck System." When you file under Birdneck's system, you identify the main topic of a document, and you file it with things that are about the same topic. Each subject gets a sticker of a different color.

MAGIC: ORANGE
Spells: sherbet
Charms: marigold
Curses: burnt umber

POOR LITTLE MOUSE SQUARE: YELLOW
Historic Sites: orpiment
Gumbling Businesses: lead-tin yellow

CUSTOMS & TRADITIONS: RED
Holiday Feszht: spice red
Poor Little Mouse Day: scarlet
Summer Flail: merlot

HORROR: BLACK
Terror: charcoal
Misc. Frights: ash gray

THE FOREST: WHITE

THE RIVER: TEAL
Commercial Trade: seafoam
Travel: turquoise

CREATURES: BROWN
Insects and Reptiles: fawn
Birds and Fish: taupe
Mammals: chestnut

THUMBKINS: PINK
Thumbkin Traditions: coral
Thumbkin Health & Safety: fuchsia
Jingle Yoinkoff: blush

THE ARTS: GREEN
Gumbling Comedy: kelly green
The Royal Gumbling Opera: emerald
The Royal Gumbling Ballet: forest green
Bards: verdigris
Folk Music: celadon
Fine Art: castleton green
Wiz Bravo: olive green

THE SCIENCES: BLUE
Biology: Prussian blue
Physics: baby blue
Engineering: sky blue
Medicine: cerulean
Alchemy: ultramarine blue
Princess Puzzline: periwinkle

HISTORY: PURPLE
Thumbkin Migration: lavender
The 1642 Invasion of Gumbling: mauve
King Lubberly I: violet
King Lubberly II: puce
King Lubberly III: magenta
Yabulga the Witch: mulberry

FOOD & DRINK: BRONZE
Traditional Gumbling Cuisine: silver
Foraging: gold

So, today, I had to file this story I copied down:

The King and the Commoner

King Lubberly III was a careless ruler. Within the bounds of his court, life was a merry whirlwind of sumptuous feasts, music, and wine, and games and treasure hunts the king designed to entertain the nobility.

Outside the castle, however, there was suffering. The poor of Gumbling had cold houses (if, indeed, they had houses at all) and little to eat year-round. It was commonly said in those times that a king could only be frightened to attention, so if you wanted him to listen, you had better use a witch. Yabulga the Witch had finally had enough of Lubberly's irresponsible ruling. So she hobbled up the hill to the castle and into the royal court. "Heed me, Your Highness," she croaked. "See that every single soul within your kingdom is fed, for if you don't, I will eat YOU!"

Lubberly did not like the idea of being eaten, so he ordered his royal advisors to think of an idea. They reminded him that after each feast and royal gala, there were piles and piles of leftovers. "Why not offer this to your people? And at two bits per plate, we could make a handsome profit!" Lubberly did like the idea of making some money off this whole ordeal, so they set out to do just that.

When they opened for business, Yabulga was the first in line. She grabbed a knife and fork and began to slice at King Lubberly. "Away, hag!" he yelped. "But, Your Highness, you did not keep your promise. Many of the good folk of Gumbling don't have the money to pay for the food you no longer want." Yabulga then went on to brag about how she would be the first witch to ever eat a king and how all her witch friends would be terribly jealous.

He begged for another chance. He ordered his royal cooks to prepare an enormous pot of mush for the town to dip bowls in, first come, first served. Yabulga just licked her lips. "By the time the old and sick get to the pot, there will be none left, Your Highness. Now, would you prefer I season you with salt or pepper?"

So, having been told that not all Gumblingers could come to the food, Lubberly had the food brought to them. Little baskets of bread and cheese were delivered to every home in Gumbling. When they reached Yabulga's door, she led the king to a boiling pot and asked him to climb inside. "You've forgotten, Your Highness, about those who have no home. They must eat, too. Now, shall I stew or poach you?"

The king paced the halls of his castle, huffing and groaning. "I'm just one king! How can I possibly ensure that EVERYONE in my entire kingdom eats?" Exhausted from all the thinking, he lay down upon his banquet table. Then he had an idea! The next morning, Yabulga came to collect her breakfast. (She thought chopped king on toast might be nice.) But when she entered the banquet hall, she couldn't find the king. Only a plain, old man. He kicked a crown over to her.

"If one man has so much, it is guaranteed that there will be someone who has nothing," he said. Then Yabulga recognized him. "Your Highness?" she snorted. "No more," he replied. "There is no more king of Gumbling and there never will be again. I relinquish my riches to feed the people of Gumbling and, from now on, the needy will call this castle home. So, you see, everyone will be fed and there will be no king for you to eat."

Yabulga gagged. A king is a delicacy, but an ex-king is very unappetizing. "You're free to go," she muttered. The king left the castle and lived happily ever after.

I liked this story better than the giant baby one, at least. But here's the problem. Under the Birdneck System, it could be filed under King Lubberly III, Yabulga the Witch, or Food. I didn't know where to put it. So I asked Birdneck, and she said I can make three copies and put one in each section.

I said, "Where's the copier?" and she held up a MIRROR.

"You are the copier."

Brrrrrrrgghhh. She was serious, you know. She's so old-fashioned that everything has to be done by hand. It's a pain in the neck. And the wrist.

And can someone tell me the difference between celadon and verdigris??? I'm an artist and I don't even care! This woman is making me hate COLORS.

Anyway, soon I'll be spared. Tomorrow's the last day of my apprenticeship before winter break. Two whole weeks without Birdneck. Pure happiness.

I went upstairs to pick up Myra from the town council office. It looked like she was doing the exact same job at her apprenticeship as I was: just filing a ton of paper.

We walked to the Third Wish and got some hot chocolate. This is the kind of thing we'll get to do every day over the holiday. Just hang out. No worries, no obligations. I'm so excited.

She does this sometimes. It's not my favorite thing about Myra. She's really good at fixing her own problems, so she's not very patient when other people aren't as fantastic as she is.

Ugh. Then she acts like such a sweetie pie when she gets her way. I love her, but come on, Myra.

Then again, if there were a time to park my attitude, it would be Feszht. Feszht is a time to feel happy and good. I will box up my anger and put it away. That should work.

HAPPY FESZHT!

Dear Journal,

When I woke up, I smelled hot eye rolls. They sound creepy, but they're actually really tasty, and Dad makes them special on Feszht.

It's a spiraled-up pastry topped with sour cream, and you can put anything circle-shaped on top of that.

Rib likes ham.

I like an egg.

Schmitty and Pa like jam.

Dad likes olives and peppers.

When you finish putting everything on, it looks kind of like an eye. It symbolizes the eye that's been watching over you all year.

Huh. Maybe that is kind of creepy. But they're still really good.

When I got downstairs, Rib was taking the rolls out of the oven, and Dad was already boiling an egg especially for me. It almost made me cry. I think the holidays make me so happy that I'm actually a little sad. Feszht is supposed to do that, anyway. It's all about thinking back on the last year and what you lost, what you gained, and what you got to keep.

I'm thinking about my year so far. Sure, I lost my chance to apprentice with a real artist and I have the worst job ever, but I got my own new room, and I got to keep my family and friends. I guess it evens out. I'm not going to dwell on the stuff that bugs me. I can't! It's Feszht!

Sometimes being the oldest is kind of a burden.
But I'm remembering what I'm thankful for today.

I'm thankful that school was so easy today. You know how it is the day before vacation. Everyone's all excited and distracted, and nothing really gets done. Myra doesn't like it as much as I do.

I value my education! Why are we even here today if everyone's basically already on vacation?

I dunno.

Gil's just been nibbling at an eye roll I brought for him all day. He likes jam, too.

Leabelle made everyone these really pretty cards. I don't get it. I've barely had any time to draw the past couple of weeks, and she's turning out these gorgeous, delicate little masterpieces, even though she's been spending all her afternoons doing art with Wiz Bravo. He's probably teaching her all kinds of new painting techniques, too. These are so pretty. I hate them.

HAPPY Feszht!

To: Nell
From: Leabelle

What is she? Magic? I'm not joking. That's very possible.

Voila handed out cards, too. They were more like advertisements, really. Her mom, the "talented and esteemed singing star" Bahbra Lala, is doing a performance at the Feszht tonight, and Voila's going to sing a song with her.

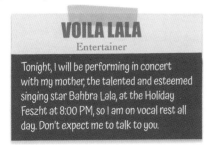

VOILA LALA
Entertainer

Tonight, I will be performing in concert with my mother, the talented and esteemed singing star Bahbra Lala, at the Holiday Feszht at 8:00 PM, so I am on vocal rest all day. Don't expect me to talk to you.

This is the one time Voila is totally quiet. I couldn't help it. I laughed a little. Then she shot me a glare. That said a lot.

School got out, and Myra and Gil went to their apprenticeships right away. When I got to Rib's classroom to pick him up, he was sitting on the floor, reading one of his big spellbooks. I had to call his name a couple of times, and then I went to sit down with him. That got his attention.

Schmitty was outside, rolling around in the snow. I predicted she'd be super energetic because little kids always get lots of candy at school on Feszht, but I didn't know she'd be this bad.

She begged for a piggyback ride on the way to the CMCC. She fell asleep by the time we got to the castle, which just made her deadweight on my back. Since you're my journal, I know I complain to you about my little siblings a lot, but I'm actually a pretty good big sister, and I love them very much.

I hope this goes okay.

Dear Journal,

Well! Pa was wrong. Birdneck didn't care that it was Feszht at all.

Or, at least, she wasn't exactly understanding about me bringing Rib and Schmitty to the archives.

I thought you had realized by now that these are very precious and sensitive documents. This is not a playground.

I know, I know. But I told my dads I'd watch them. And Rib is a really good boy. And Schmitty ... well, she's asleep, so she can't do anything destructive.

You should have made other arrangements. I expect any apprentice of mine to respect these archives and respect my rules.

That made me mad. It's not like I asked to babysit. I'm being responsible for my family and, hey, I think I'm demonstrating pretty good character. But all she cares about are her pointless archive rules.

I rolled my eyes. I couldn't help it. She made my eyeballs so mad, they just went off on their own! Then she sort of smirked, like she had known I was going to do that. I clenched my fists and felt my nails dig into my palms.

As long as you're already on vacation, you might as well skip off to the party now.

I've been working really hard here, and she never even says thank you. I was boiling. So I said something I probably shouldn't have:

It doesn't make a difference whether I'm here or not.

I beg your pardon?

You don't even want me here. You just make me do all this busywork, and none of it even matters!

Well, that's fine, because I don't want to be here, stuck with some uptight old robot who cares about rules more than people!

(So much for boxing up my anger.)

She was reeeeeaaaally quiet. She was that painting in a haunted house all over again.

The only thing I heard was a whimper. It was Rib. He was acting like he was the one in trouble. I had honestly forgotten he and Schmitty were there for a second. I had forgotten everything except being mad for a second.

Then she took a breath.

I think it would be best for you all to go now.

... I'm sorry.

That is quite unnecessary. Enjoy your vacation.

I actually was kind of sorry. I don't know if she knew I meant it. I picked up Schmitty and we all got out of there.

Schmitty woke up while we were going upstairs.

Aww! I missed the dungeon??

I messed up. Even though it was snowing out, my entire body felt hot. Except for my stomach, which was ice-cold.

Rib could tell I was upset. He hugged my whole arm. He's been doing that since he was a baby. It's really sweet.

Schmitty's approach was more direct.

Did you get fired?

No. Maybe. It's a volunteer thing for school. I don't think I can get fired.

Does this mean you're not gonna be fun tonight?

That question was like an electric shock. Just because I'd had a weird, terrible moment didn't mean I had to bum out the people I was with. I tried my best to shake it off. I couldn't let this ruin my Feszht!

No way, you goose! Let's go!

THE GUMBLING HOLIDAY FESZHT

Hot Lullipeach Cider
(Pa always gets a big mug of the
fermented cider. It's for adults only.
They can keep it. I took a sip once, and
it tasted like there was something
wrong with it. Blegh.)

Third Wish
Fairy Teas

Soupman Garlic's
Wonderful Soups

Thumbkin
Pies

FISH
HOUS

FOOD & DRINK
STALLS

Candy and
Spiced Nuts

GAMES &
ACTIVITIES

Treasure
Hunt

Ring Toss

Fishing
Game

The Gumbling Folk Band plays and there's dancing.

Bahbra Lala's Feszht Concert (the one Voila is in)

ENTERTAINMENT

Puppet Theater (Every half hour, they do a puppet show, "The Legend of Feszhtmama.")

Puzzline's Carousel (We always go here first.)

First: the baby activities. I have to admit, I still love the Feszht stuff for kids. I always liked it when I was little, and since I have younger siblings, I get to keep doing it without someone like Voila Lala making a snobby comment about it.

Okay, this one's really cool. It's this hand-carved, hand-painted amazing machine from two-hundred-something years ago. Back then, Princess Puzzline, the princess of Gumbling, was an engineer, and she built these wooden automatons. She wanted to make something special for the children of Gumbling, so she made this carousel.

On the inside, it runs on clockwork. (They opened it up for us to look at in school last year.) On the outside, there's a real working clock in the middle, then a calendar outside that, and then a ring of wooden animals you can ride outside that. They're all native animals of Gumbling, which means Schmitty HAS to go multiple times so she can ride all her favorite animals. And the carousel also plays Feszht music through a wooden pipe organ inside the machine. I'm not the most science-y person, but I think it's all pretty interesting.

Then we hit the five-thirty puppet show. It's about Feszhtmama, who's the hero of Feszht (like they have Santa Claus for Christmas in other places).

The legend is about this nice old lady who never had any children, but who took in all the poor orphans and the mistreated children of Gumbling. She would take her magic eyeball out of her head and roll it away. It rolled all over the kingdom, looking for children who needed her. She'd invite them to live in her safe, warm cottage, where she would always take care of them.

Again, I know the eyeball thing sounds weird and gross, but I read that the original story of Santa Claus was that he found these three pickled children (some guy was going to sell them as hams) and brought them back to life. So I think old stories are just weird and gross sometimes.

Then I took Rib and Schmitty to meet Dad and Pa at the mouse statue. They were sharing a cider and listening to the band.

Myra was at her mom's stall. She was stirring a steaming pot with all these flowers sticking out of it.

I had fairy tea when I had a bad fever last year. It really does make you feel better. I thought some tea might help me feel better about my Birdneck problem, but I didn't see anything on the menu that would do the trick.

We found Gil at the Thumbkin pie stand with his cousins.
His whole family loves goofing around, so they're lots of fun.

In the wintertime, fairies wear these knitted wing-covers.

I put my hand on the table so Gil could climb up, Then all his little cousins started to crawl up, too, and Gil's mom had to come over and peel them off my arm.

We hit the cider stall. Then the plan was to get some soup and split a Feszhtmama cake.

At the soup stand, we saw Ms. Garlic. I know seeing teachers outside of school is supposed to be very disorienting, but we get soup from Ms. Garlic every Feszht. It's kind of a tradition. Her family's been making famous soups forever, so they have all these special recipes.

my favorite

MENU

Sour Lemon
and Dumpling Soup

Traditional Dinghy Putt

Garlic's Cream of Pepper
(our oldest family recipe)

Ten Bean Soup

Poor Little Mouse
Pumpkin Bisque

Pirate's Salt Pot

Fire Noodle Soup

After Myra and Gil got theirs, they went to sit down. I stayed for a while after Ms. Garlic ladled my soup.

... Something on your mind, Nell?

Not exactly. I mean, yeah, kind of.

Then I asked something I didn't want to ask. I didn't want to be like Voila and try to weasel out of my apprenticeship just because it was hard. But being a lorekeeper, Birdneck, all of it—I just couldn't take it anymore.

Ms. Garlic . . . is it too late to switch apprenticeships?

She took off her apron and asked her brother to take her place at the stall. Then she came around and sat with me.

Hmm. Well, we can certainly talk about it. What's going on?

So I told her everything. How I had been dreaming about apprenticing with Wiz Bravo and I didn't understand why I got matched with Mrs. Birdneck. How I've been trying my best to do a good job at the archives. How Birdneck was so tough on me. The hardest part was telling her about my outburst this afternoon. I said I was pretty sure Birdneck was going to call her and ask for a different apprentice anyway, so I was just letting her know now. She smiled and looked at me.

I'm going to tell you why I paired you with Mrs. Birdneck, okay?

When I was in seventh grade, I apprenticed with Mrs. Birdneck. She was tough on me, too. And I wasn't expecting it. She was married to my homeroom teacher, Mr. Birdneck. And he was such a sweet man. I didn't know why his wife was such a grouch.

And I didn't even last as long as you. I think I asked him about two weeks in if I could switch apprenticeships. But he really encouraged me to stick with it and find where I connected with lorekeeping.

So I tried to have a little more patience with Mrs. Birdneck, and I ended up really valuing her style of teaching. It's not the way I teach, but she pushed me and helped me a lot. She was the one who helped me find my family's old recipes in the archives.

I could tell underneath that hard shell, she believed in me. And we actually became good friends.

That's really nice. I just don't know how I could ever face her after today.

I think things are a little tough for Mrs. Birdneck lately. Mr. Birdneck passed away around this time last year, and she's still grieving.

She wasn't even sure she wanted to have an apprentice this year, but I told her I was sending her a really special one.

...Me?

That's right. I think you can help each other out a lot, Nell. You're so bright and curious, I thought lorekeeping would be a perfect fit for you. And I see what a kind friend you are in class. I thought Mrs. Birdneck could really use an apprentice as cool as you.

But I'm not going to force you to go back. We can work something else out, and you can start with a new mentor in January. Do you have any ideas?

I knew she meant it, that I could start over. I know Ms. Garlic—she's not trying to make me feel guilty or anything. She always tells the truth.

But I don't think I want to start over. If Ms. Garlic is telling the truth (she is), then all that stuff about Birdneck is true, too. And if it is, then I guess I don't want to give up.

Maybe I can just try to start fresh with Mrs. Birdneck in the new year?

Are you sure?

Yeah. I want to try.

Good for you, Nell. But this is on Mrs. Birdneck, too. A good apprenticeship should involve mutual respect.

Thanks.

Then we said "Happy Feszht," and I went to meet Myra and Gil for cake.

I hope Ms. Garlic's proud of me. I'm kind of proud of myself.

We got our Feszhtmama cake and went to grab good spots for the concert. My family had saved some for us.

The concert began. Bahbra Lala has one of those voices where... I don't know how to explain it, but moms can't get enough of it. You look around while she's singing, and all the moms in the crowd are swaying and getting really into it. I saw Mrs. Didwell shed a single tear. Dad ate it up, too.

But for my taste, it's a little slow and boring. Like, she does all the soulful, ballad-y Feszht songs, you know, like "Feszht Is in Your Heart" and "The Greatest Gift Is Love." And they're soooo sappy. I guess they're good for showing off a spectacular singing voice. But there are so many FUN Feszht songs you could do: "Uh-Oh! Feszht Is Here!" or "Mama's Magic Eye" or "Four Little Gumblebuns." And anytime she DOES do a fun song, she does a slowed-down, boring version. What a waste.

Ugh. And when she called up Voila to do their duet (they did "It Won't Be Feszht Without You"), Voila curtsied and did this fakey-fake smile, like "I'm the most darling girl ever." And the whole audience went "Awww." It was so gross.

Then something absolutely wild happened.

Because who should walk onstage but those two out-of-towners—
Wet Nails and Teeth. They were clapping and walking the Lalas
offstage. Then they came back to the microphone, and a
projection screen came down.

Thank you so much, ladies.
What a special, unique
performance. Wow.

We want to thank you all for
a lovely evening. What a warm,
welcoming little hamlet this is.

I looked at Myra and
mouthed "Why are they
talking?" She shrugged.

I'm Tom
Greatman-
Bigby!

And I'm his
sister, Christina
Greatman-Bigby!
And we're . . .

THE LOST
PRINCE AND
PRINCESS OF
GUMBLING!

The crowd fell silent. Was this a joke? Or, like . . . a skit?
A couple people laughed.

I know it sounds funny. Believe me, we were pretty surprised to find out we're royalty, too. After all, we're just a couple of venture capitalist's kids from New York City.

When we read on HuntMyAncestry that our great-great-great-great-grandfather was Lubberly III, king of Gumbling, we were like, "Whoa. Us?"

But as soon as we set foot here in Gumbling, it all started to make sense. We felt an instant, unexplainable kinship with the people. We felt the majestic beauty of the land and culture wash over us. And we knew . . . we were home.

And we know we're not the only ones who are going to feel that way. Gumbling is an irresistible place to visit. I don't have to tell you all that it is literally magical. And we want to share that with the world.

That is why we're using our royal birthright to do something incredible. Not just for Gumbling. But for anyone who's ever needed a little magic in their life. That is why we proudly present . . .

CASTLEWORLD!

This time I actually heard some gasps. Some were like you-just-slapped-me-in-the-face gasps and a few were like ooh-tell-me-more gasps. Either way, they did tell us more.

Great Big Developers has traveled all over the world, developing luxury resorts and must-see travel destinations.

Diamond Towers. The Grand Caligulan. The Coconut Breeze. It's what we do.

And this time, it's personal. We're putting Gumbling on the map, baby!

People all over the world will now have premium access to their wildest fairy-tale dreams.

They'll get the royal treatment when they stay in a one-of-a-kind luxe suite in our fully refurbished castle.

They'll dine in kingly elegance at one of twenty signature restaurants.

And as for entertainment, they can take in a Broadway-style show, have a virtual adventure in our state-of-the-art VR chamber, or even ride our . . . roller coaster.

A couple kids in the crowd gasped for the roller coaster.

For the first time in history, these guests will have the keys to the kingdom.

They will be able to go on enriching learning excursions to explore the fascinating culture of this land.

And children will have the time of their lives meeting your tiny folk and seeing real live fairies and unicorns.

We're bringing Gumbling to the world by bringing the world to Gumbling!

I looked over at Myra and Gil. They were stunned.

... What?

Oh no no no.

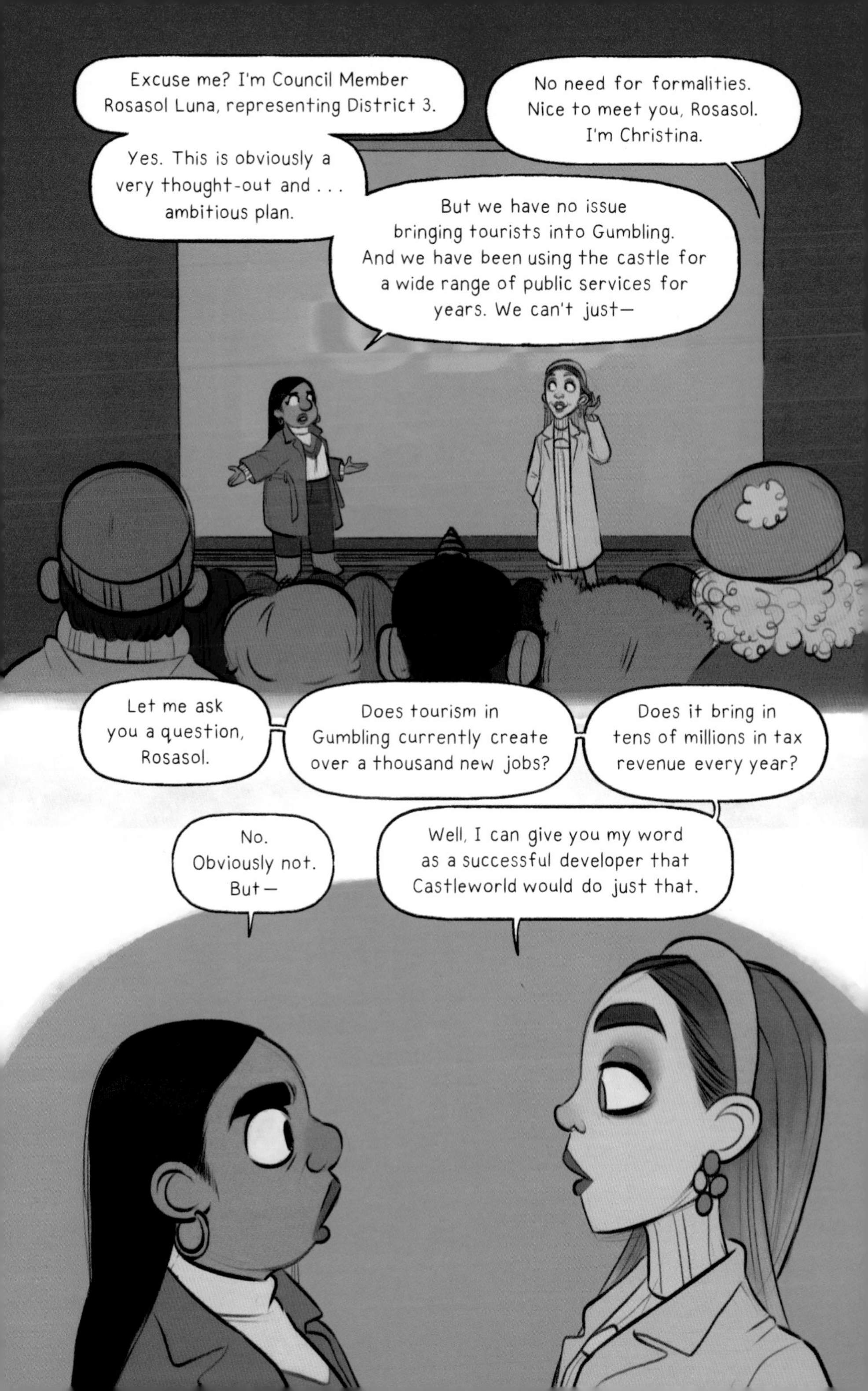
Excuse me? I'm Council Member Rosasol Luna, representing District 3.
No need for formalities. Nice to meet you, Rosasol. I'm Christina.
Yes. This is obviously a very thought-out and . . . ambitious plan.
But we have no issue bringing tourists into Gumbling. And we have been using the castle for a wide range of public services for years. We can't just—
Let me ask you a question, Rosasol.
Does tourism in Gumbling currently create over a thousand new jobs?
Does it bring in tens of millions in tax revenue every year?
No. Obviously not. But—
Well, I can give you my word as a successful developer that Castleworld would do just that.

Listen. We know this is a new idea. And new ideas can be a little scary.

But let me assure you, we want to work with the people of Gumbling to ensure that this project is designed to everyone's satisfaction.

And let me assure you: this is not something Gumbling needs.

That's your opinion. But I'm sure there are other opinions. And personally, I believe that our royal ancestors would want Gumbling to live up to its potential. That's something Castleworld can deliver.

We're going to make this happen. After all, it is technically our castle.

We'll see about that. I call for an emergency town council meeting tomorrow morning. It will be discussed.

Then the Great Big Developers packed up their presentation and left the stage. The crowd kind of dispersed, and people packed up their stalls. It was a . . . weird vibe. After all, massive resorts and emergency town council meetings aren't exactly in the spirit of Feszht.

This is some kind of hoax. Why would anyone believe these people are who they say they are?

If they are, that's gonna put the council in a tight spot. The town has to warmly receive any and all children of Gumbling. It's in the town charter or something.

What does that mean? They're actually going to be the new prince and princess?

No way. The last king of Gumbling said there wouldn't be any more kings when he left. He said the castle was for everybody.

Gumbling wouldn't return to a monarchy just because two scam artists say they have a claim to the throne. It can't.

But are they going to make Castleworld?

No.

No. I don't think they can do that. That castle is a public good. We all use it. For Pete's sake, people live there. They can't take that away now.

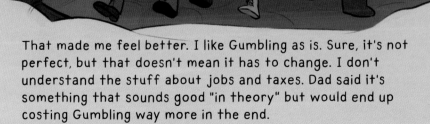

That made me feel better. I like Gumbling as is. Sure, it's not perfect, but that doesn't mean it has to change. I don't understand the stuff about jobs and taxes. Dad said it's something that sounds good "in theory" but would end up costing Gumbling way more in the end.

It's a lot to think about. And my head hurts.

Dear Journal,

It's winter break!!! After all the drama yesterday, I'm looking forward to two weeks of total rest and relaxation. So I went to see if Myra wants to go ice-skating.

I had to bundle up pretty good, because it snowed all last night. That's okay—I like wearing my bundles in the snow. They're cushy.

Rib was outside practicing a color-changing spell on some rocks. He's been studying his spellbooks so much, but now that he's actually trying to do magic, it's not going that well. Poor Ribbo.

Schmitty's bummed out because her favorite Hoofbeast, Big Girl, went into hibernation with her herd yesterday. She tried to get Schmugly to come out of his coop to play, but Schmugly doesn't like the cold. Poor Schmitty.

Too bad for them. But I was going to have a wonderful day!

But when I got to the Third Wish, Myra wasn't there. Her dad said she was at the council meeting. Funny thing to do on your first day of vacation, but also very Myra.

When I went to the CMCC, she was already sitting up in the balcony overlooking the council meeting. She waved me over.

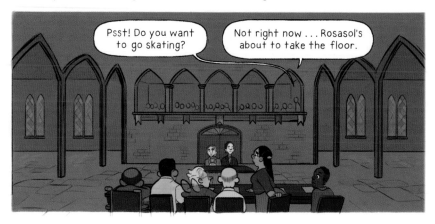

It was me and Myra and a bunch of grown-ups who kept nodding and then shaking their heads and going "Hmm."

I don't really understand a lot of the words they were using. It just sounded like a lot of political gumblejumble to me. Myra said there are two big things they're arguing about:

1. Are the Greatman-Bigbys actually descended from King Lubberly III? Do they have any right to say what happens here?

2. Would Castleworld be a good thing for Gumbling or not?

She said Rosasol takes a firm stance on both issues. She thinks Castleworld would be terrible for Gumbling, and she doesn't think it even matters if they're descended from royalty or not. We don't think so, either.

The problem is, there are a couple of other people on the town council who like the idea of the town getting more money from tourism, and one guy keeps bringing up ancient laws from the town charter that say we have to treat these "children of Gumbling" with respect, especially since we don't even know who the castle legally belongs to.

But we do know. The castle belongs to the people. That's what the last king said.

Yeah, but he just said it and disappeared. It's not in any official document, so it's not legally binding. It's a loophole.

I hate loopholes.

Me too.

So I basically understand what's going on, but I zoned out when they droned on about all the provisions and subsections of the town charter. I know it's important, but it's also BORING. And it was no better when the Greatman-Bigbys took the floor. I yawned, and Myra shot me a look. So I tried to swallow the rest of my yawns.

Wait, so are they still staying at the Third Wish?

No, thank goodness. They're leaving town for a while so they can "get a decent Wi-Fi signal." But they said they'd be back.

When they opened the floor for public comment, I nudged Myra to say something, too. But she was feeling too shy.

Well, that was super dull, but at least we'll do a real day of winter break tomorrow.

Dear Journal,

Well, Myra went to watch another council meeting today. She says it's her civic duty. I want to be a good citizen, too, but I only have so many days before I have to go back to school and Birdneck, and I reeeeeaaaally wanted to go ice-skating.

So, I went ice-skating. I'll do my civic duty some other time. Myra gets it. I hope.

Gil and I went to the pond. It's all frozen over now and perfect for skating. For Feszht, his grandma made him this little chair with a seatbelt and an adjustable strap on the bottom that we can buckle to my shoulder. It's supposed to be a lot safer than just sitting on my shoulder. He says it's pretty comfy, too.

What do you think of the whole Castleworld thing?

The roller coaster sounded cool. But I don't think I'd be able to go on it. I'm only tall enough for shoulder coasters like you.

Plus, you know how my mom feels about tourists.

Oh yeah.

Whoa.

Gil was looking at Leabelle (obviously). She was skating in the middle of the pond, and she was doing all these jumps and twirls. Why are some people just good at EVERYTHING?

Come on, let's go tell her you're in love with her.

NELL! SHUT UP!

I'm kidding!

We skated over to Leabelle and some of the kids from school. They were talking about Castleworld, too.

My dad says it would bring the town so much money. We could get more computers for the school and stuff.

All the new restaurants sound good, too. Anyone else kind of sick of eating soup all the time?

Mom's adoring fans would love to see her perform in a world-class venue that's actually worthy of her talent.

85

I still think I'm right. But I don't feel smart. Voila has a way of doing that. Sure, Castleworld might bring some money and excitement to Gumbling, but at what cost? The businesses and dignity and homes of our friends and families? Shoot. That was kind of good. I should have said that.

Leabelle was really nice, though. She showed us how to do spins. I think Gil nearly swallowed his tongue, she was near us for so long.

More stuff I've done on winter break:

Watched movies
with my family

Made snowpeople
with Myra and Gil

Ate every new
recipe Rib tried out

Colored with
Schmitty

Read two books
and lots of comics

Forgot to write in my
journal (oops, sorry)

HAPPY NEW YEAR!

Dear Journal,

Tonight Dad and Pa went to a New Year's Eve party at the Third Wish, so I babysat Rib and Schmitty. Schmitty and I drew, and Rib made macaroni and cheese for dinner.

You're going back to your job this week, right?

Oh . . . yeah . . . I haven't thought about it all holiday.

If the lady makes you mad again, just spit on the ground. It always works for me.

Thanks, Schmitty.

Then Rib put this handful of dust in the macaroni.

Rib! What are you doing?

It's just jemmy flakes! Hoofbeasts eat them all the time. You won't even taste them!

What did you put them in for?

It's a tip from my spellbook. Jemmy flakes combined with Hoofbeast milk, which is in the cheese, are supposed to bring you good luck in the new year.

Okay. But it won't do anything weird to us, right?

No. Definitely probably not.

Here's hoping that Rib's magic macaroni works! I need all the luck I can eat if I'm going back to Birdneck this week.

Dear Journal,

It's the first day back at school. I picked up Gil, and we went to the Third Wish to get Myra. She gave us these buttons.

When we got to school, some kids frowned at our buttons. Voila said, "Très clever slogan," all sarcastic.

Leabelle took a button and asked if she could help make more. I wish I'd said that first.

Myra's all fired up about going back to her apprenticeship. She and Rosasol are going through the town's laws to find a way to fight back against Castleworld.

I wanted to get fired up, too. Have a good attitude. And hopefully, nothing would mess that up.

After school, we parted ways at the castle. I made my way down the spiral staircase, but something was different. Usually it's closed and so dark down there that I have to feel around for the doorknob. But today there was light coming from the bottom of the stairs, and when I got there, the door was propped open.

Nell? Is that you? Come in.

The dungeon looked so different. I mean, not SO different. There were just some lamps set up and a couple of space heaters. But it made a difference. And I want to be different, too. I want to have a good attitude.

Happy New Year, Mrs. Birdneck. I like the . . . light and heat.

Yes.

Um . . . I'm really sorry about what I said last time.

Ahh, yes, when you called me a . . . What was it? "Uptight old robot."

You called me impudent and silly and lazy first! And I said I was sorry.

I heard you. And it's a new year. We can consider it in the past.

She said it was in the past, but it didn't feel true. I was grumpy, but I still felt like apologizing, but then I was nervous she'd hate that—if I just kept saying sorry. That's probably bad manners or something.

Ms. Garlic feels I haven't been engaging you in the lorework enough.

Yes, and now I'm talking to you. You're bored and unhappy. Why?

. . . She talked to you?

I don't know.

You seemed to have plenty to say when you spoke with Ms. Garlic.

It was like she was yanking a tooth out of me.

It's just . . . the work I do here . . . the vacuuming and copying and filing . . . it can be kind of tedious. I don't think I'm wrong for thinking that.

It's noble work.

Cleaning ensures you are respectful of the space.

Copying down texts multiple times cements the content in your memory.

Filing under the Birdneck System strengthens the mind's organizational skills.

Okay, then. I'm sorry I was lazy. I'll just be . . . more noble or whatever.

I am not looking for an excuse or an apology. I am looking for a solution.

If copying down texts and filing doesn't interest you, what would?

Huh?

Don't stand there gulping like a fish, girl. Do you have interests or don't you?

I can't believe Ms. Garlic thinks I'm ever going to get along with this woman.

She just walked up to the second level of the archives and disappeared. I was so confused.

When she got back, she was carrying this big stack of folders and books. She laid them all out on the table and set one huge, thick book right in front of me. She opened it up.

The original lorekeepers in Gumbling would create rich, lovely pictures to go along with the histories they documented.

Oh . . .

They even had pages written on dyed paper in an ink that could only be read under starlight.

I imagine they're a good deal more complex than the comical books you enjoy, but you may take a look, if you'd like.

The book was open to the history of Princess Puzzline. I had only seen her inventions before. I'd never even seen her portrait.

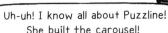

Princess Puzzline

You likely don't know who this is.

Uh-uh! I know all about Puzzline! She built the carousel!

I see. Well, then, you might occupy yourself with these as well.

Then she pulled out a bunch of documents about Puzzline: a biography, letters between her and other scientists, even some of her journals with designs for inventions.

So . . . you want me to copy these down?

That will be unnecessary. Just see that they're returned to their proper places when you're finished looking at them.

Really? I can just look at these?

You're of no use to me in the archives if you're going to pout and make little effort. But I suppose I can't expect you to feel anything for this lore if you can't explore it yourself first.

Then she went back to her desk. I had the whole afternoon to myself with all this stuff.

Okay. I don't believe this myself. But it was actually pretty fun, looking at all that Puzzline material. I kind of understand how Myra feels when she's doing a deep dive into local law or how Gil feels when he's doing a deep dive into a heap of garbage.

And for the first time in a while—definitely the first time in this apprenticeship, at least—I felt kind of inspired. Not that I'm such an important "artiste" or anything, but after looking at all this Puzzline stuff, I wanted to draw. You never know when the muse is going to strike. And it might as well strike on a day like this, when Birdneck is leaving me alone. She can call me lazy and sloppy and low-effort, but when I want to make something, I make it. So there.

If a little kid like Rib can combine his interests in witchcraft and cooking, why can't I combine lorekeeping and comics? I mean, I definitely don't want Birdneck to know I'm making my silly comics in her serious haven of historical documents. But I want to do it for me.

So I did. I drew a comic of one of the Puzzline stories and then I colored it later at home. And here it is:

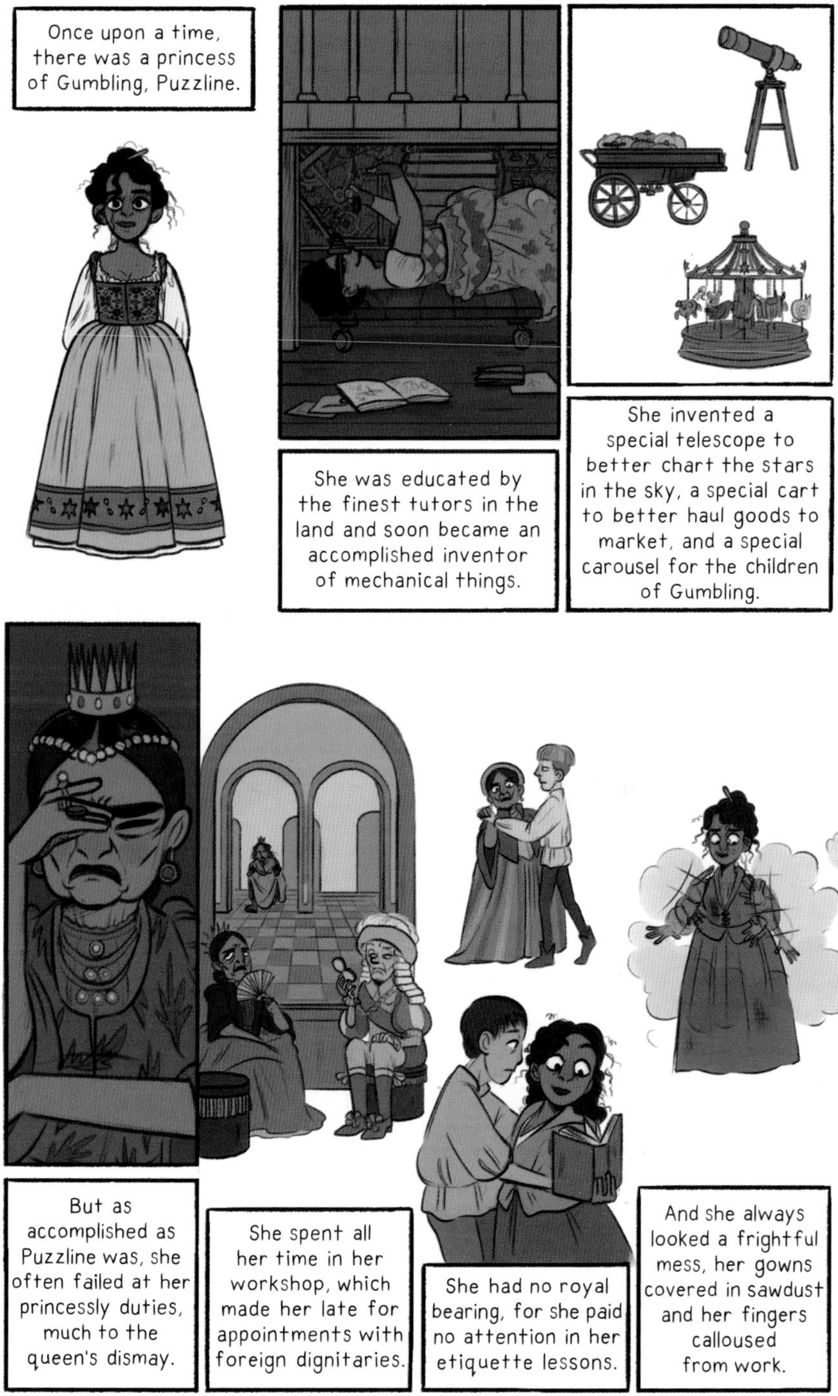
Once upon a time, there was a princess of Gumbling, Puzzline.
She was educated by the finest tutors in the land and soon became an accomplished inventor of mechanical things.
She invented a special telescope to better chart the stars in the sky, a special cart to better haul goods to market, and a special carousel for the children of Gumbling.
But as accomplished as Puzzline was, she often failed at her princessly duties, much to the queen's dismay.
She spent all her time in her workshop, which made her late for appointments with foreign dignitaries.
She had no royal bearing, for she paid no attention in her etiquette lessons.
And she always looked a frightful mess, her gowns covered in sawdust and her fingers calloused from work.

Her mother was at the end of her wits.

Enough! Puzzline, you are a princess and you have responsibilities.

This kingdom needs a princess who shows up to appointments on time, demonstrates proper etiquette, and always looks presentable.

A mechanical princess! An automated wooden princess on wheels.

None of this sounded very appealing to Puzzline. Luckily, she had a solution. So she worked day and night and built her greatest achievement yet . . .

She was built with a clock inside her so she would always be on time for appointments. Her stiff armature wouldn't allow her to slouch. She needed no sleep, so she never yawned. And she always looked perfect.

When her mother saw the cogwheel creation, she nearly fainted.

Puzzline, you are impossible! I meant I wanted YOU to be the princess the kingdom needs. Not this . . . thing.

But, Mother, this princess can do all those princessly duties perfectly. That gives me time to serve Gumbling in my own way . . .

By making star charts for our farmers and fishers, wagons for our merchants, and amusements for the children.

The queen finally understood what her daughter did for Gumbling. From that day on, she let Puzzline choose her own kind of princessly duties. And they lived happily ever after.

Dear Journal,

This is going to sound really wild, but . . . I think I figured out how to "connect" with lorekeeping and find the fun in this apprenticeship. At least a little bit. I'm gonna keep making comics!

Birdneck's been giving me a bunch more independence in the archives, which basically means we still don't talk to each other, but at least she doesn't scold me when I touch the documents now (although I do have to wear the special gloves).

Since she's not checking up on me all the time, I draw a little bit of a new comic every afternoon. They're all based on the history of Gumbling. And I use other documents in the archives to research so my drawings can be really accurate.

And I still copy down some stories and file them. (I make sure the handwriting is perfect.) I don't want Birdneck to think I'm slacking on lorekeeping. Because the truth is: I've never been more into it.

So that's been my life for the last couple weeks. I've never done an art project this big. It feels a little strange to be keeping it to myself. I always imagined being an artist would mean putting all your art out there and, you know, being famous for it. But in a way, I kind of like having these be just for me right now.

And the more I look at the history of this place, the more steamed I get that a lot of the town is even considering Castleworld. That's just not what Gumbling is. Oh yeah, remember Castleworld? It's been ruining my life all over the place.

After work, I went over to Myra's to surprise her with one of my new comics. It was my adaptation of the story of the Poor Little Mouse. Back in kindergarten, our class did a play of it, and she played the mouse and I played the pumpkin. That's how we became friends in the first place. We were backstage and she got stage fright. She was too scared to go on, so she started crying.

It's okay. You don't have to do the play if you don't want to.

I—sniff sniff—know . . .

It's just, I'm just— sniff sniff—so—sniff— GOOD AT IT! Waaahh!

H-haa- hahahhaha!!!

HAHAHhAAHAHAH!

Hee, hee hee hee hee!

So I thought she'd like to see the comic. We haven't been hanging out as much lately. She's been so busy with Rosasol, and, I don't know, it's just been harder.

When I got to the Third Wish, her dad said:

Go right up, Nell. The girls are in Myra's room.

I didn't know if he meant Myra's sister was home or what. But, when I opened Myra's door, it wasn't her sister.

It was Leabelle. They were making buttons and protest signs. But mostly they were laughing and having fun. The buttons and protest signs were just a by-product of their apparent new best friendship.

There was a pretty significant pause. I clearly interrupted a lot of fun. And I felt too awkward to stay.

I closed the door, but a couple seconds later, Myra came out and followed me.

I didn't want to look. I know I'm being a baby. I KNOW.

I know I don't have a monopoly on Myra's friendship. I know I'm overreacting. But she obviously knew I would have feelings about this, because she didn't want to tell me. So . . . it's not like I'm in the right here (I'm literally never right when I'm having a fight with Myra), but I am hurt. And that's not nothing, is it?

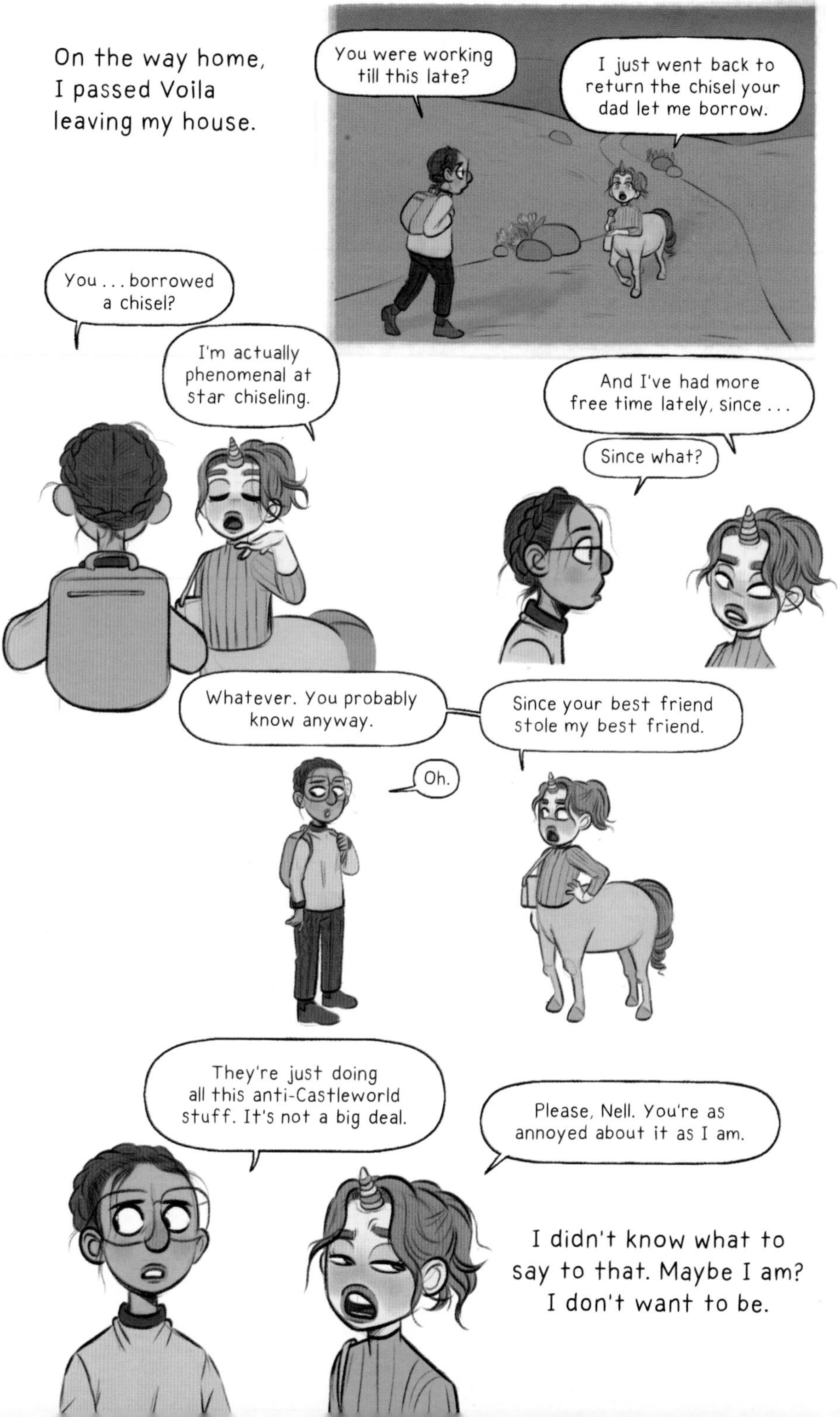
On the way home, I passed Voila leaving my house.
You were working till this late?
I just went back to return the chisel your dad let me borrow.
You . . . borrowed a chisel?
I'm actually phenomenal at star chiseling.
And I've had more free time lately, since . . .
Since what?
Whatever. You probably know anyway.
Since your best friend stole my best friend.
Oh.
They're just doing all this anti-Castleworld stuff. It's not a big deal.
Please, Nell. You're as annoyed about it as I am.
I didn't know what to say to that. Maybe I am? I don't want to be.

She kept going, and I walked to the house. Rib and Schmitty were on the porch.

I sat by the door and eavesdropped.
(Yeah, I KNOW it's a bad habit, but . . . I did it.)

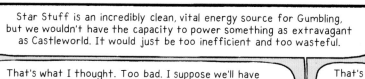
Star Stuff is an incredibly clean, vital energy source for Gumbling, but we wouldn't have the capacity to power something as extravagant as Castleworld. It would just be too inefficient and too wasteful.

That's what I thought. Too bad. I suppose we'll have to call in a few favors and set up our own power grid. Good luck hanging on to your farm when we do.

That's ridiculous!

We're just being practical. We need power that your little star system just can't supply.

It's sad. You're not the only business in Gumbling that won't cooperate. We have to bring in all-new food suppliers, energy, merchandise, entertainment, a security force. It's really a shame.

So you've just come here to threaten us.

Well, duh.

It's fine. We don't want anything to do with your business anyway. No one in Gumbling is going to stand for it.

Kindly get out of our home.

We all scooted out of the Great Big Developers' way. They didn't even see us. Schmitty and Rib were still a little scared to go inside, but I went in.

Oh, Nell, there you are.

Hiya, gumblebun.

Were you really going to work with those people?

Not really. We wanted to see what we were up against. Now we know.

They want to put us out of business. They want to put everyone in town out of business.

Don't scare her, Malloughby.

It's okay. I know what's going on. I went to a council thing with Myra.

But I didn't know it was getting this serious. And bad. I wish I could do something. Myra's at least trying. But I don't think she wants me to get involved.

I'm no good at this kind of political stuff.

I don't really understand all the legal speak, either, pumpkin.

But the first step to getting involved is caring. And it sounds to me like you care a whole lot what happens to our town and the people in it.

And maybe this is Myra's forte. But everyone's got something to offer. Don't forget that.

The only people who win if we feel too shy or too unqualified or too unimportant to fight are people like the Greatman-Bigbys.

I guess you're right . . .

I'm happy Dad and Pa trust me enough to talk to me about this kind of stuff now that I'm old enough. But it's also hard to hear. I don't want them to worry about the farm, about taking care of us. I want to take care of them, too. But I feel too little. "Old enough" and "too little" feel like the same thing to me right now.

I'm guessing you're not feeling your best today?

Yeah, sort of.

Do you want to talk about it?

I don't know. Maybe.

Okay. Well, Rib made cookies. Do you want to cookie about it?

Hee hee hee, sure.

Pa always knows how to make me feel a little better. I don't know how he does it, but he knows.

Is it about you and Myra?

Should I try to help, or should I just listen?

Just listen.

I wish I knew how to keep up. Myra's so good at her job, and she loves it so much and it's inspired her to take action with all the Castleworld stuff.

She's so put together, and it makes sense that she'd be friends with Leabelle now because Leabelle has it all figured out, too. Like, they're just two people who are good at everything and know what they want.

I feel so left out.

And Gil's great but he can't be my best friend.

And Voila doesn't have a best friend anymore, but I don't want to be her best friend.

It's like I wish I could go back in time, back to before the apprenticeships and Castleworld and everything, but I wouldn't want to take all this new stuff away from Myra because it makes her happy.

I just want to stop feeling jealous and bad.

That's not as easy as you want it to be, huh?

Nope.

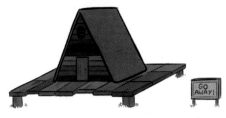

Dear Journal,

Today was kind of wild. I mean, home and school were normal enough. Even though I didn't talk to Myra. I kind of wanted to, but she didn't talk to me first. You know how it is.

Then when I got to Birdneck's, she was locking up the dungeon.

We're going on a field trip.

We are? Where?

We're picking up some very unique books from a friend of mine.

So we walked up the stairs and out of the castle. It was nice being outside, with the snow melting and the sun out. I'd never seen Birdneck in natural light before. She looks less like a scary wax figure.

But I started to get scared all over again when we entered the forest. That's when I realized where we were going.

This is the way to . . . Yabulga's hut, isn't it?

That's right.

I gulped. It's not that I'm afraid of Yabulga, exactly. I mean, if Birdneck isn't scared to go over there, I shouldn't be. But then I remember that children are always told to stay far away from her hut or something bad will happen. And I remember that she said she was going to eat the king. And . . . I'm a little scared.

Birdneck must've sensed that I was nervous when we got to Yabulga's moldy, mossy door.

Mercy, girl. Stop shuddering. She won't turn you into a frog.

I've specifically asked her not to.

When Yabulga opened the door, the first thing I noticed about her was that she wasn't there. She was way, way across the room. She must've enchanted the door open.

We went in, and she puttered over to us. She was really small—she couldn't have been more than four plunks tall. She stood right in front of me and squinted.

You're at odds with someone very important to you. And you like Feszht eye rolls with a soft-boiled egg on top.

Huh?

Yaba. No mind reading, if you please. It's rude.

Sit, sit. The tea will get cold.

When we sat down, Yabulga's cat jumped on my lap.

The cat was really warm. You could feel her ribs, but her tummy was still big. And she didn't have a lot of fur. She was almost bald in some places, like she'd had a bad haircut.

Any news from the outside, then, Birdie?

Nothing you'd like, I'm afraid. The council is still considering the developers' proposal.

I ought to eat the both of them.

Oh my gosh.

Oh, it's a joke! No one gets my jokes. But it worked when I told that Lubberly I'd eat him, didn't it? Haven't had a single rotten king since. Till these so-called royals waltzed into town with their stinking hotel idea.

Can't you do something about them, Yaba?

You don't think I'd like to? They're playing a different game, Earla. My tricks don't work as well as they used to, not in this modern world.

I'm old and tired. Getting King Lubberly out of the castle was my last great triumph, and that was a hundred blasted years ago.

Besides, that was a . . . What's the word? A "freebie." I only had to use my wits. No magic.

Most societies have to rise up in revolution to depose a king. But this one was like a jar someone already loosened. He was ready to go.

Did you ever see him again?

Only one more time, and that was quite enough. The fool. Talking some gumble jumble about leaving a bequest. "What bequest?" I said. "You're not the king anymore! Go away before I eat you."

If you keep saying you'll eat people and never follow through, it's going to lose some of its power.

You're probably right. Anyway, I'll get you those books.

She snapped and a couple of marked-up spellbooks from her personal collection floated over to us. Birdneck says she donates them to the archives every once in a while. And then we left.

On the walk back to the CMCC, I was thinking about Myra. We always said we were going to be best friends until we were old ladies. So I guess seeing old-lady best friends sort of reminded me of that. It's not that deep.

So . . . how long have you and Yabulga been friends?

Ages, it seems. But then again, we often go a long time without seeing each other.

Doesn't that make it hard to be friends?

We are two women with very different lives. I have little interest in her witchcraft, and she has no interest in my archives. So we spend much of our time apart.

Two people needn't be in total sync to be close. What a childish notion.

"Childish." Hmph. What does she know about friendship? It's probably been a million years since she had a sleepover. And besides, it's important to share things with your friends.

Myra and I have always had a lot in common. We both like flowers and reading and pretending and puzzles and . . . I mean that's all little-kid stuff that we liked when we were little. Now I guess I like

comics, and she likes her job and her activism and all this important stuff that I'm not really a part of anymore. Maybe we're more like Birdneck and Yabulga than I thought. I don't believe you can still be best friends if you've grown apart so much. That doesn't make sense. But I miss Myra a lot, too.

I can't wait to tell Rib about this. He's not going to believe I met Yabulga. Don't get me wrong, it was pretty creepy. I've read all these stories about the spells she casts and the curses she places, and she's not someone I would want to push too far. But she was also a tired old woman who feels kind of powerless now. I felt kinda sorry for her. Or, at least, more sorry than scared. I wonder what she meant about Lubberly's bequest . . .

Dear Journal,

I saw Myra walking to school this morning. She looked too wiped-out to fly. Like, really super tired.

She took a big breath, and then she told me.

She didn't sleep at all. The developers came back yesterday, and her room is right next to the room where Christina Greatman-Bigby's been sleeping. So last night, Myra overheard her talking to some investor on the phone. (Yes, again, eavesdropping isn't perfect or whatever, but it can be VERY effective.)

So she was saying, "No, of course this is on the up-and-up. We're the lost heirs to the throne. That castle is practically our property. We could probably sue THEM for using it for a hundred years without our permission."

Oh, come ON.

And then she said, "We've been buttering up the town council, and we've got a few in the palm of our hand. Some were easy. That Rosasol Luna's a real thorn in my side, though. Maybe we can find a way to get her recalled."

No way.

Yes! I'm telling you, Nell, I called it. They're straight-up evil.

Well, what can we do? I want to help.

No, you don't.

I do. You haven't really given me a chance to try yet.

Of course I did. You were just being stubborn.

Well, you were, too.

Okay. I know we're not perfect right now. And I know I'm not as good at this as you are. But the only people who win if we feel like we can't fight back are the Greatman-Bigbys.

You have a point.

If you want to help, that'd be cool.

"Leabelle and I." That's Myra's new unit. It used to be "Nell and I." But I can't get jealous. I want to be friends with Myra again, and I want to help her do this. So I'm just going to put that jealousy away. Fold it up all tiny and swallow it.

Okay. Scrap that, then. We're looking for documents?

Yes. There's got to be some kind of paper trail they've left behind. Some evidence that they've been playing dirty.

I'll go through the garbage from the Third Wish!

Can you really do that?

I dunno. But who's gonna catch me? I'm tiny!

And I'll dig deeper into the laws at the town council office. There has to be some ordinance those scumbags are violating. I'm gonna take them down.

And I guess . . . there's probably nothing helpful down in the archives.

That's no kind of attitude. Maybe you'll find something down there.

Or you can . . . help Leabelle and me make stuff to protest at the council meeting tomorrow? Offer moral support?

Yeah. Totally.

Get pumped! Get motivated! Get mad! We're gonna do this.

Okay, okay! OKAY! I'll do my best.

So, I went down to the dungeon after school, feeling a little useless. When I got there, Birdneck was at her desk, looking at a scroll with her superfine magnifying glasses.

What are you looking at?

Lenore, please. I am trying to concentrate on something very important, and I do not need any distraction.

Whatever. Can't be helpful out there. Why would I be helpful here?

She sat up straight. Then she spun around and took off the glasses.

And what, pray tell, does that mean?

Nothing. Never mind.

Commit, child. You had the thought. Now finish it.

It's just . . . ugh. I want to help take down Castleworld, and I can't.

And I'm not complaining about being bored, I swear. The lore's actually been somewhat, kind of, sort of interesting.

I want to do something for the cause, but all I can do is shuffle papers around down here.

Your enthusiasm is staggering.

But I wish I could do something to make a difference.

And lorekeeping doesn't make a difference. It's not important.

I didn't say that.

I've heard it before. And many a time, I've thought it myself. After all, who really cares about this clutter from the past when we'd like to charge ahead into the future?

I shouldn't've said anything. I'm sorry.

I know children don't care about our history.

I know I'm partly to blame. Children don't like me very much.

That's not . . . um, totally true.

I'm not a fool, Lenore. I've always wanted the children of Gumbling to see the lore as I do. As vital, relevant, and crucial to understanding who we are and where we come from. But their parents hardly see it.

And why should they? History won't put food in their families' stomachs. It won't keep those bloodsuckers from taking our castle, our homes, and our jobs, and writing their own history of this place.

Do you know what I was looking for when you came in?

All night and day, I've been trying to find anything in my documents that could save my library. Any protections against the destruction of the archives.

Those Great Big Developers said this would be the perfect place to put a twenty-four-hour fitness center.

What?

If they have their way, I'll be sent out of my library and my home.

My whole life is here. And who will care? Who will even remember?

I am invisible.

A nuisance.

Easily disposed of.

Gee. I think I just saw Mrs. Birdneck break.

She started to cry a little bit. I felt so awkward. And sad.
I handed her my sweater to wipe her eyes.

Hmm. Thank you.

I would care.

I wouldn't want the archives to disappear. They mean something to me.

And even if they didn't, I would want them to stay. Because they mean everything to you.

I think I actually saw her smile at that one. Will wonders never cease?

I grabbed her glasses and held them out to her.

Birdneck put the glasses back on and faced the desk. She took a big breath.

I climbed up the stairs and into Cell 3, where Birdneck puts all the spillover documents that haven't been filed yet.

I picked through a pile of incredibly random papers. Some records of trade between Thumbkins. A handwritten pamphlet of fairy lullabies. A newspaper from the day Snowbilly Mim and Primbilly Mum were born. But nothing that would solve our problem.

Woof. I leaned back against the cell wall.

Now, I probably wasn't supposed to do that, because the wall turned all the way around and spun me around, out of the dungeon.

I ended up in a laundry room. And I couldn't find any stone to press to turn the wall back around.

As far as I could tell, this was in the housing part of the castle, where people live, not the administrative part, where the archives are. I was nowhere near the archives anymore.

Shoot. I was lost.

Just then I heard soft footsteps. Someone was coming in.

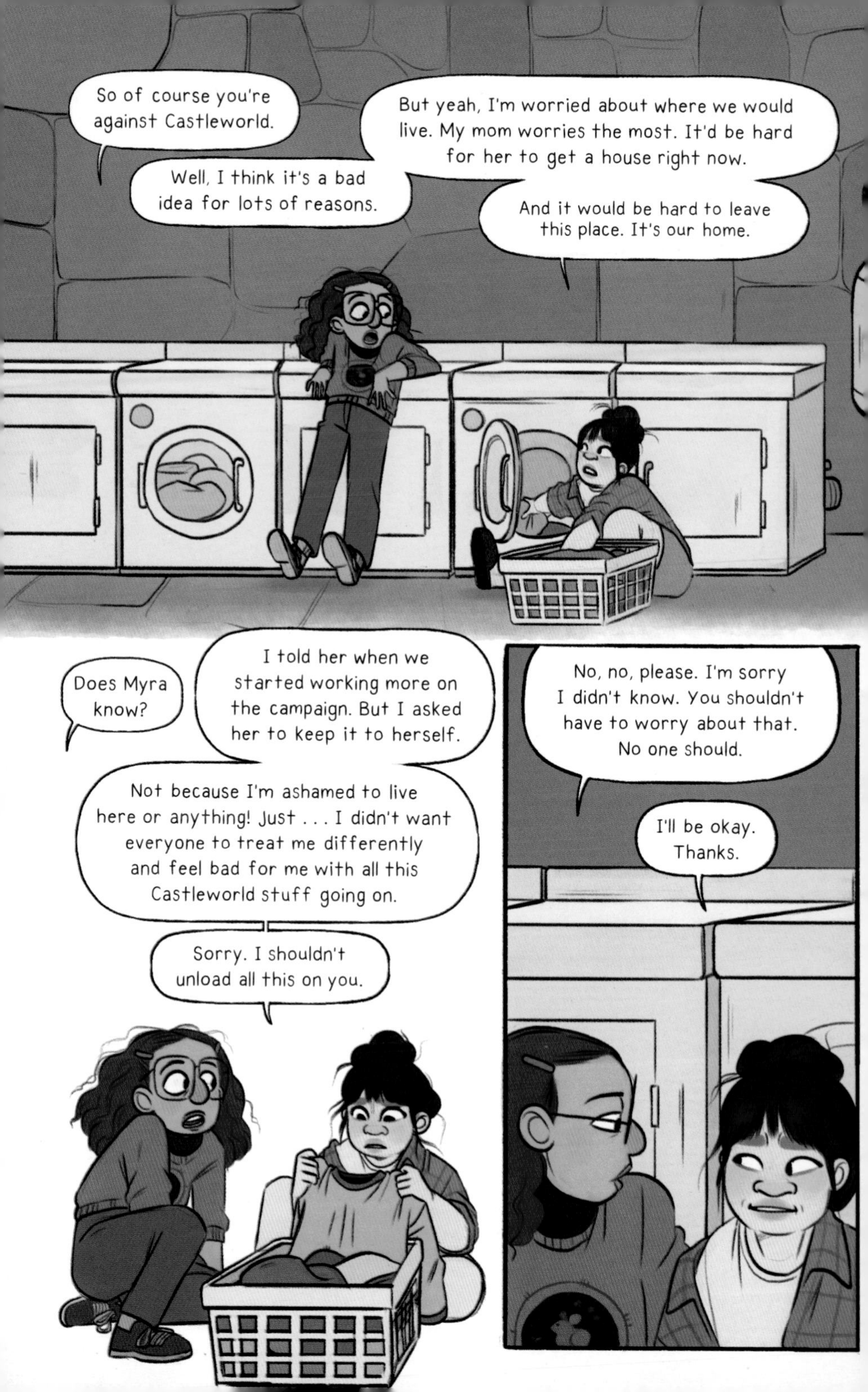
So of course you're against Castleworld.
Well, I think it's a bad idea for lots of reasons.
But yeah, I'm worried about where we would live. My mom worries the most. It'd be hard for her to get a house right now.
And it would be hard to leave this place. It's our home.
Does Myra know?
I told her when we started working more on the campaign. But I asked her to keep it to herself.
Not because I'm ashamed to live here or anything! Just . . . I didn't want everyone to treat me differently and feel bad for me with all this Castleworld stuff going on.
Sorry. I shouldn't unload all this on you.
No, no, please. I'm sorry I didn't know. You shouldn't have to worry about that. No one should.
I'll be okay. Thanks.

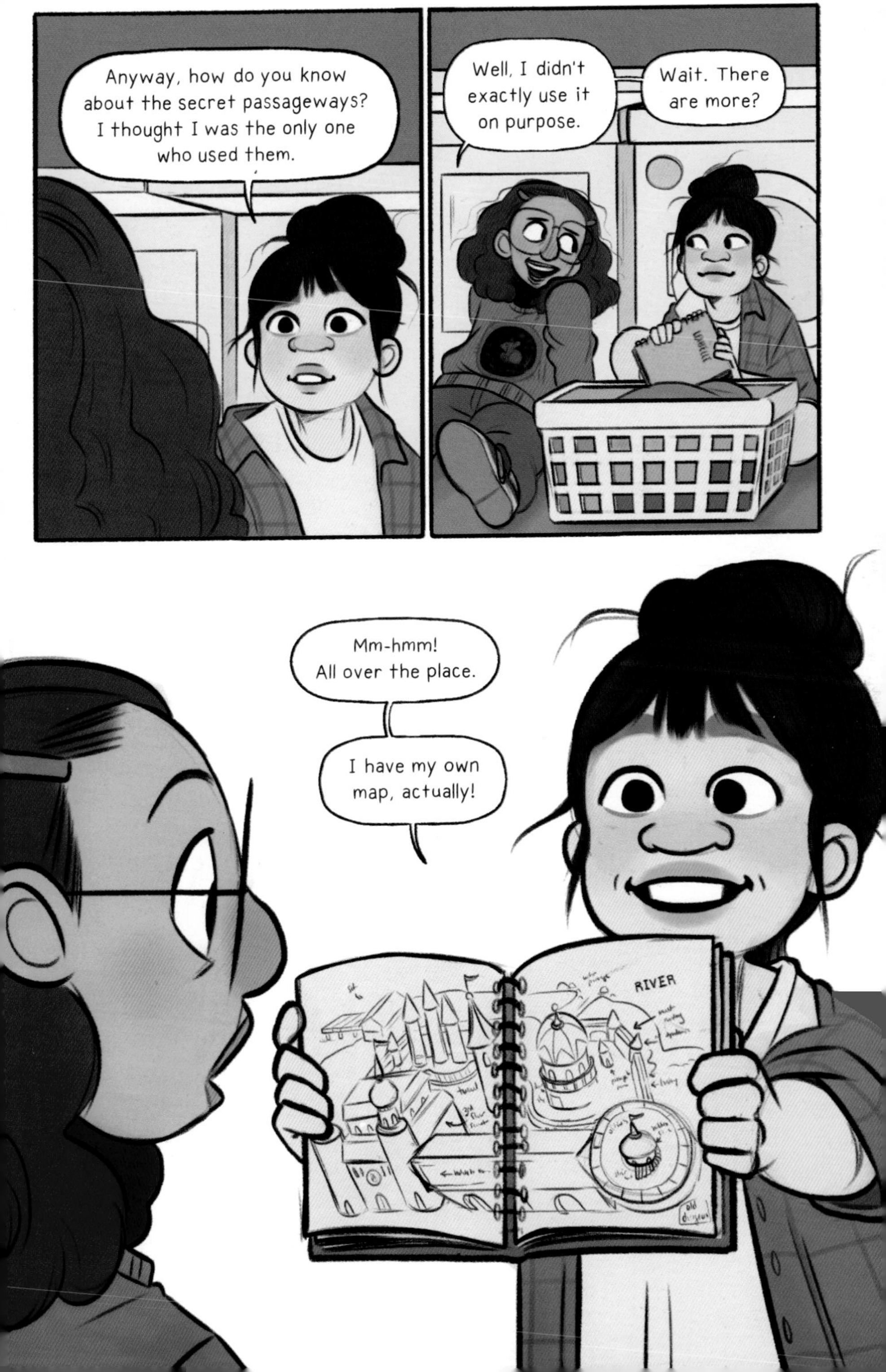
Anyway, how do you know about the secret passageways? I thought I was the only one who used them.
Well, I didn't exactly use it on purpose.
Wait. There are more?
Mm-hmm! All over the place.
I have my own map, actually!
RIVER

This is so cool! And it's really beautiful! You showed this to Wiz Bravo, right?

Isn't he supposed to be your mentor?

I just help him with his projects. You know. Washing brushes. Sharpening pencils. Getting him coffee.

Oh. No. Mr. Bravo is never really interested in seeing my drawings. He's busy with his own art.

What?

It's not that bad. It's just . . . not what I thought an apprenticeship with my hero would be like.

It's not what I thought it was, either. Honestly, I envied you.

Really?

Uh-huh. Big-time.

Well, I guess you're not envious now. Of a bored brush-washer who's about to lose her house.

Well . . .

I'm kidding.

I'm still really envious of how talented and pretty and nice and smart you are and how you never smell bad, if that helps.

You know, it kind of does.

Then I told her how I was trying to find the ex-king's bequest to stop GBD from building Castleworld. But it was impossible because Lubberly left the castle and the kingdom without a trace.

Oh, he didn't leave the castle.

. . . Huh?

At least, I don't think he did.

She led me down the hall, to her family's apartment. We went into her room, and she sat me down on the floor.

Leabelle pointed to a brick in the wall. It had a name scratched into it: Herdburt Blithely.

She opened her sketchbook and scrawled down the name, and then she mixed up the letters and . . .

But what does it mean?

I don't know. Do robot mice mean anything to you?

Huh?

Leabelle knocked on the Herdburt Blithely brick, and it popped out of the wall. That must have triggered something, because a moment later, this little wooden mouse on a spring popped out of the hole. It fidgeted, made a squeaking noise, and then popped back in. Then it came back out and did it again. Like a cuckoo clock.

HERDBURT BLITHELY

And that's all that ever happens.

Is that anything?

Huh. I don't know.

The mouse looks like something Princess Puzzline made. You know, like the carousel.

She handed me the brick, and I shook it. It sounded hollow, so I felt around for any irregular patches. This one part felt uneven, like a notch. And when I pushed against it, the brick opened up, and a scroll rolled out.

Here it is:

If you seek the key to Gumbling, then, child of Gumbling, heed:
Look first from the tiny place where I was trapped and freed.

We ran back to the laundry room, and Leabelle showed me how to get back through the wall. (You had to pull on a sconce.) I rushed from the spillover archives into the main library and ran all the way up to Birdneck.

I caught Myra and Gil at the Third Wish. I told them about the brick and Leabelle's genius letter-scrambling and the mouse and the scroll and everything.

It's not like either of us found anything today. I'm in.

Come on, Myra. We're not going to get anywhere without you.

Fine. But if it doesn't work, I reserve the right to say "I told you so."

I can accept that.

Great. But no one tell my mom. She says treasure hunts are the leading cause of injury in children aged nine to fourteen.

Dear Journal,

Today is the big day. For a lot of reasons. Today we're going on our quest to find the key to Gumbling. But it's also a big day for a bad reason: tonight is the town council meeting where they'll officially decide if Great Big Developers can do Castleworld. But we're going to stop them. We're going to get the key.

I met Myra and Gil in Poor Little Mouse Square.

So what now?

There's nothing there.

We search over there. The statue of the Poor Little Mouse.

The clue didn't say look "at" the place where he was trapped and freed. It said to look "from" it.

How are we supposed to do that? We can't get in there. It's tiny.

I'M tiny.

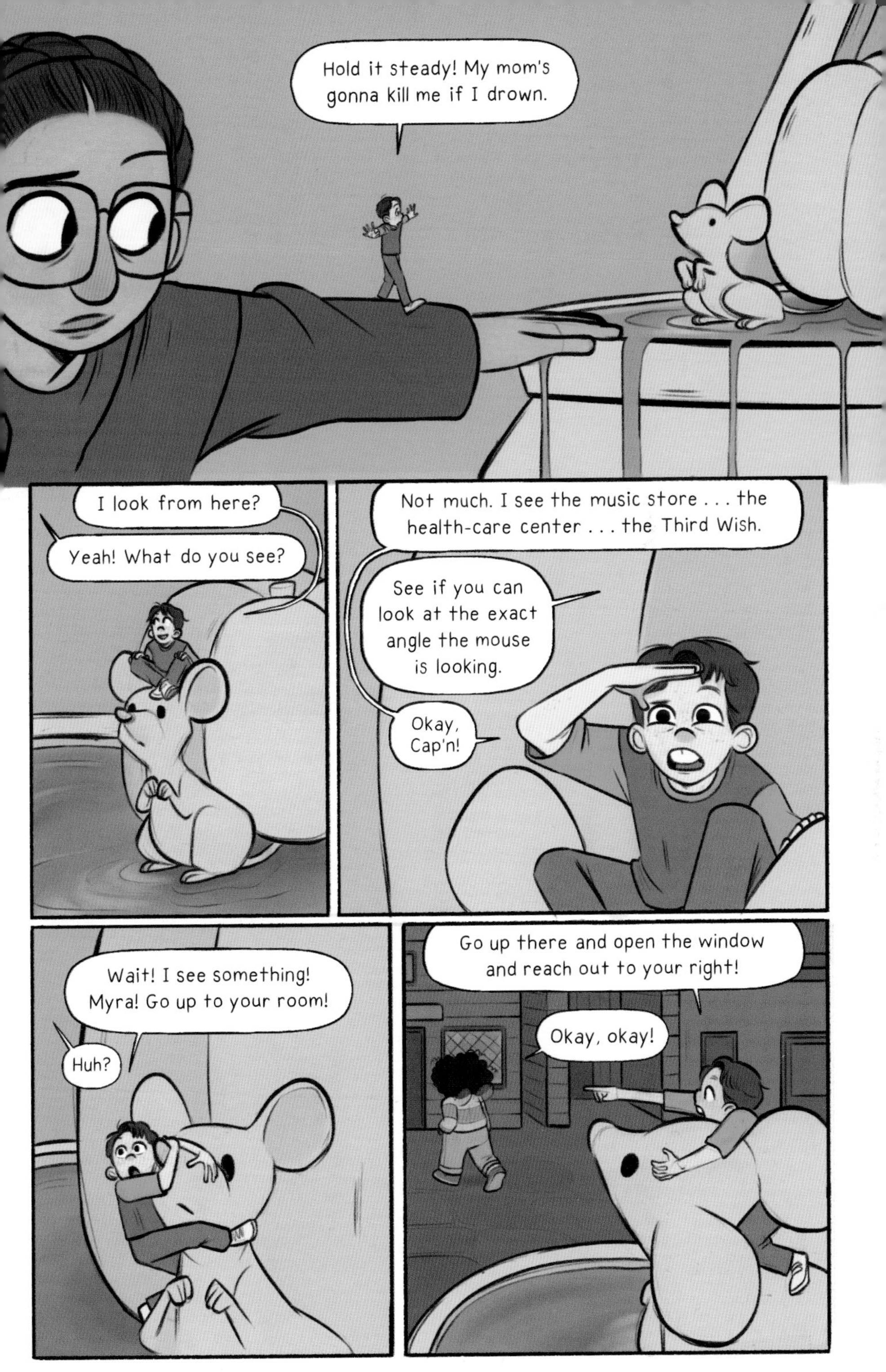
Hold it steady! My mom's gonna kill me if I drown.
I look from here?
Yeah! What do you see?
Not much. I see the music store . . . the health-care center . . . the Third Wish.
See if you can look at the exact angle the mouse is looking.
Okay, Cap'n!
Wait! I see something! Myra! Go up to your room!
Huh?
Go up there and open the window and reach out to your right!
Okay, okay!

Myra went inside and reappeared at her window. She reached and felt the edge of a pocket in the wall.

Whatever this is, I can't get it from here!

So Myra climbed out the window and got her wings going. I'd never seen her fly this high! She grabbed something in the pocket and flapped over to us.

Whew! Good thing I've been working these bad boys out.

Myra, YES! What'd you find?

It was a little statuette of
the Thumbkin from the story,
Jingle Yoinkoff, pointing
at the mouse statue.

There was another scroll tied around Jingle's leg:

Now from a former ruler's throne
May you behold the purple stone.

Purple stone,
huh? Is that
from a story?

None I can
think of.

I think—nah, that
wouldn't work.

What is it? There are
no bad ideas right now.

All right,
let's go.

We ran (well, I ran, Myra flew, and Gil rode on my shoulder) to the CMCC. Myra led us to the town hall, where they do the council meetings and hearings.

This is where the throne room used to be, back when there was a king.

But there's no throne to look from. And I don't see any purple stones.

Amethyst is a gemstone, and it's purple. Maybe that's what he meant. Are there any crown jewels around here?

Purple stone . . . purple stone . . . purple stone . . .

Eureka!

I knew if I kept saying "purple stone," someone would get it.

Myra went over to the window and drew the curtains to let in the light. There was a huge stained glass window, and it cast colorful light all over the floor.

She smiled. Maybe that means she likes me a little again!

So we combed the floor until we found one stone that was completely covered in purple light. We pried it loose. There was a glittering gold chain with a locket hanging from the bottom of the stone. When we opened the locket, there was a scroll inside, but this one was on black paper. There wasn't any writing on it.

Dead end.

Maybe not. Nell, let me see that locket again.

She showed us the front of the locket.

Just as I thought! There's no such thing as a dead end for a Didwell, Gilligan.

See, I thought I recognized a fairy glyph. That's the symbol of Centaurus, the Star Fairy.

So we have to go find him now?

No, but it must mean the clue has something to do with stars.

Nell, what do you think?

Me? Well . . . it kinda reminds me of these dyed pages down in the archives. You can't see the ink, because it's special.

Sooo . . . ?

I think we have to read this scroll under starlight.

Maybe we don't have to wait . . .

We don't have time to wait until it's dark to read this! We'll miss the town council meeting!

We hustled over to my house. Pa was in the star patch.

Pa! We need a fresh star! It's so we can save Gumbling.

Whoa, Nelly. Slow down. You can have a star, no problem. In fact, this is a perfect opportunity.

Voila! You wanna put on a show for the folks?

Oui, certainement!

And then something unbelievable happened. Voila Lala galloped off the porch and did a bunch of pirouettes and leapt onto the lift. She did this whole big production as she rose into the sky and picked a star, then descended and twirled off the lift. She trotted over and handed us a fresh, sparkly star.

I gave my dad a confused look.

Et voilà! I guess I'm amazing at farming, too!

Once she put her own spin on it, she was the fastest learner I've ever seen. Good work, Voila.

Naturally.

So we huddled up to read the clue under the starlight. But then Voila butted her horn in.

What are you even doing?

We're on a mission to find the key to the kingdom and stop Castleworld.

But you wouldn't be interested. You've already made it very clear you want Castleworld to happen.

Oh, that? I changed my mind.

But I thought you wanted your mom to do their shows?

Those GBD ghouls were very rude to dear Maman, actually. They want to do some tacky show with a "name" artist-in-residence instead. They make me ill.

So you're only against them now that it personally affects you?

Yes, obviously.

That checks out.

Anyway, I guess I can come along on your little quest thing.

Did we invite you?

We might need her. Look at this clue.

Your search proceeds, your quest moves on, to the point of Zhizhelle Montbonbon.

I had to copy down the story of Zhizhelle Montbonbon, like, five times. She was a famous ballerina who used to dance at the opera house. So I think we have to go there.

And I know every inch of that theater. I was practically raised in it.

Okay, Voila, you can come.

You're welcome.

So we made our way to the opera house, with four new (and unplanned) guests.

Voila led us through the back entrance and into her mom's dressing room. Then we went through a narrow hallway, up some stairs and past some velvet curtains, and we ended up onstage.

Gil's minuscule voice bounced off the walls, all the way to the back of the theater. There were at least five "hello"s. Then someone out at the back of the house turned around.

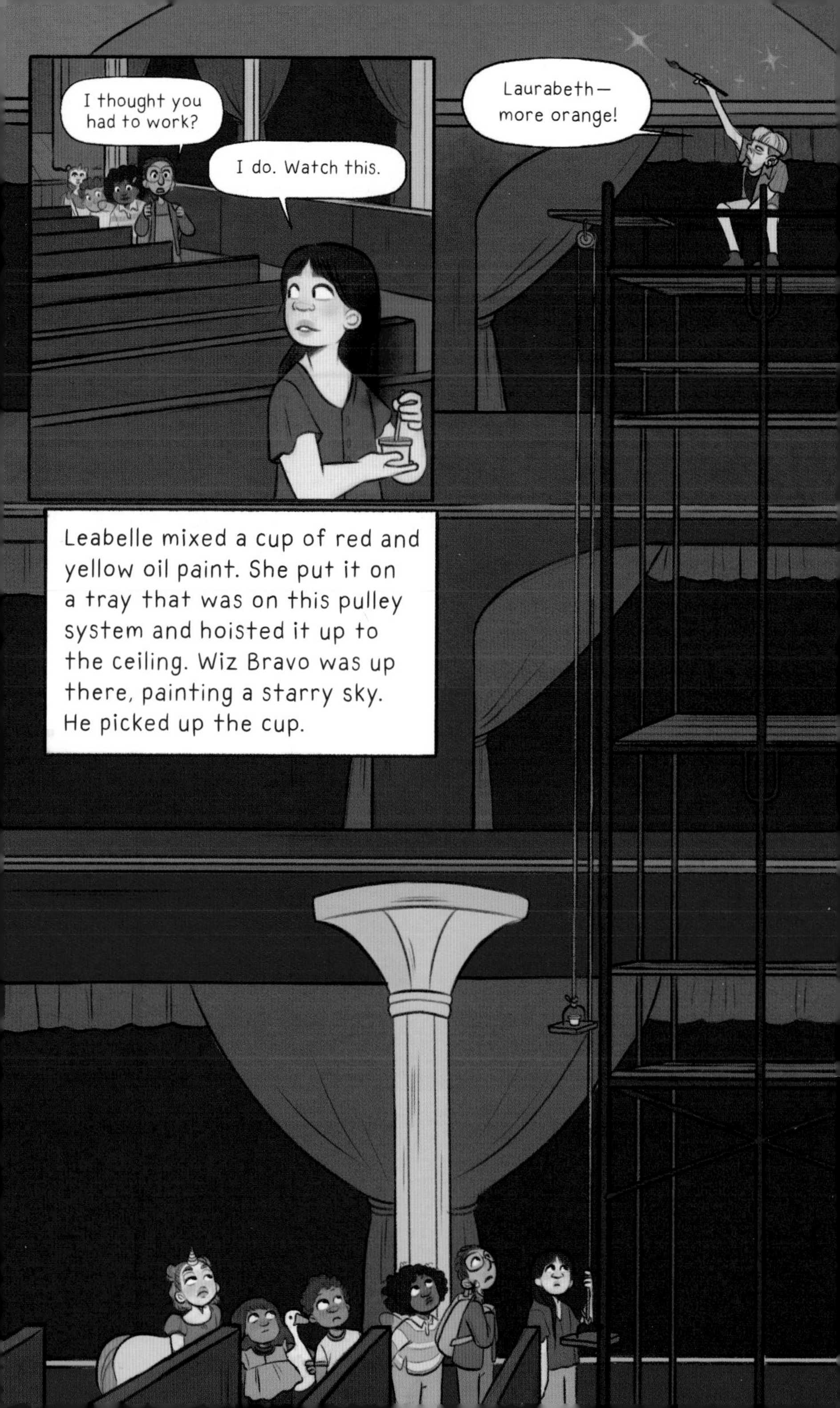
I thought you had to work?
I do. Watch this.
Laurabeth—more orange!
Leabelle mixed a cup of red and yellow oil paint. She put it on a tray that was on this pulley system and hoisted it up to the ceiling. Wiz Bravo was up there, painting a starry sky. He picked up the cup.

It's lumpy, Lilabrie.

Does he know your name?

He's gotten close a couple times. How's your thing going?

We're still hunting clues, but I think we might actually find the key to Gumbling.

MAYBE.

They're making more progress now that I'm with them.

We're looking for something here in the opera house. You should come!

I guess he's not going to notice if I take a teeny-tiny break.

Do you know where we could find Zhizhelle's Point?

Hmm . . . come with me.

She showed us out of the theater and into the lobby. The walls were painted with a mural of the story of Zhizhelle.

She walked right up to one part of the painting. Zhizhelle was kind of gesturing to her fiddle guy.

This is the painting he did in the fall. The one I was telling you about. See how it's kind of like a comic?

She could be pointing, right? "Zhizhelle's Point"?

It couldn't be that.

Nell, don't be rude!

I'm sorry. I thought that might help.

No, no, it was a good idea. It's just, if Lubberly set up this hunt a hundred years ago, we can't look at a clue from last year. It's got to be older. Like some artifact . . .

That makes sense. Well, there's lots of old stuff around here.

Then Voila started giggling.

What's funny?

Ohhh, nothing. I just happen to know where to look.

WHERE?

Come, come!

She waved us over to a glass display case. Inside were the magical ballet shoes and fiddle.

See, this ex-king was either trying to be clever or he was really bad at spelling. He said the next clue was at Zhizhelle's Point.

Voila opened the display case and pulled out the shoe.

But he meant Zhizhelle's pointe.

As in her pointe shoe. I'm an entertainer. I know all the vocabulary.

153

She pulled another scroll out from behind the insole.

Et voilà!

Though shoes and fiddles aren't the same,
Go back to the place whence we came.

"Whence"? What's a "whence"?

It means "from where." We're looking for the place the shoes and the violin came from.

But they come from entirely different places. Shoes are made by cobblers, and violins are made by luthiers.

Do you know EVERY word?

But they've got to have something in common. Because both the shoes and the violin were magic.

That's right! They were enchanted, so every time Zhizhelle danced or the fiddler played, they'd be transported to this theater! But what made them magic? A potion? A spell?

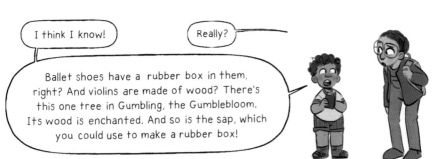

Rib pulled out his <u>Pocket Encyclopedia of Magic</u> and flipped to a page in the middle.

Leabelle peeked inside the theater. Wiz Bravo had his headphones on. He had no idea she was even gone.

She thought for a second.

So we ditched the opera house and went up the hill and over the bridge to the southern bank of the Gumbling River, right across from the CMCC. Myra kept checking her watch.

There were lots of trees, but only one with a sloping trunk and pink and white blossoms.

We got to the tree, but there weren't any notes anywhere.

I climbed up to see if there were any clues hanging from the branches. Nothing (except I got a new scrape).

Come on, tree!

We dug up the dirt all around the base. Nothing.

Gil wandered around to the back of the trunk, where there was this really big knothole. He stepped onto the edge of it.

Maybe there's a clue stuffed in here!

Aaaaaaaaaaaaaahhhhh!!!

Oh no!

So Myra flew down to go grab him. A moment later she came out with Gil in her hand.

So apparently this tree is an entrance to the catacombs. It's dark and creepy, but what we're looking for is probably down there.

Are you all right, Gilligan?

Uhhhhh . . .

He's fine. Before he could hit the ground, his shirt caught on this.

EW.

Cool!!

Augh!

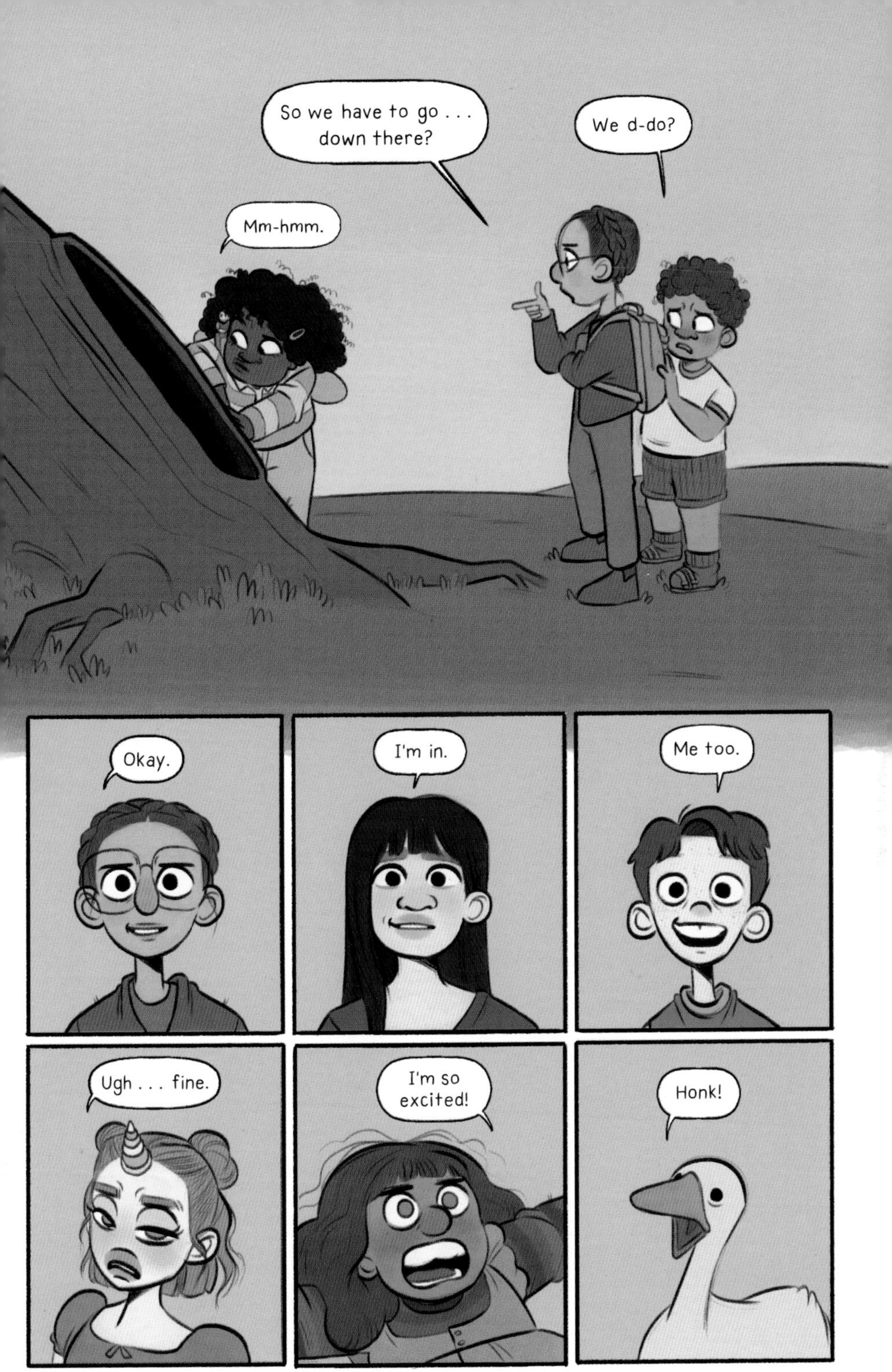
So we have to go . . . down there?
We d-do?
Mm-hmm.
Okay.
I'm in.
Me too.
Ugh . . . fine.
I'm so excited!
Honk!

Myra flew Gil down first. Leabelle slid down after. Then Voila went down, trying not to touch anything. Myra flew back up for Schmitty.

Now it was just me and Rib. He was trembling.

I'm not gonna make you go in, buddy.

But everyone else did . . .

You don't have to be everyone else. You've already helped a lot today. You got us here.

If we do go in, I promise I'll take care of you, and I'm gonna help you if it gets scary. But you don't have to go.

Will it be really dark?

Maybe, but guess what? I've still got my charging star.

Rib had some little tears balancing on his bottom eyelids.
He wiped them off on his shirt.

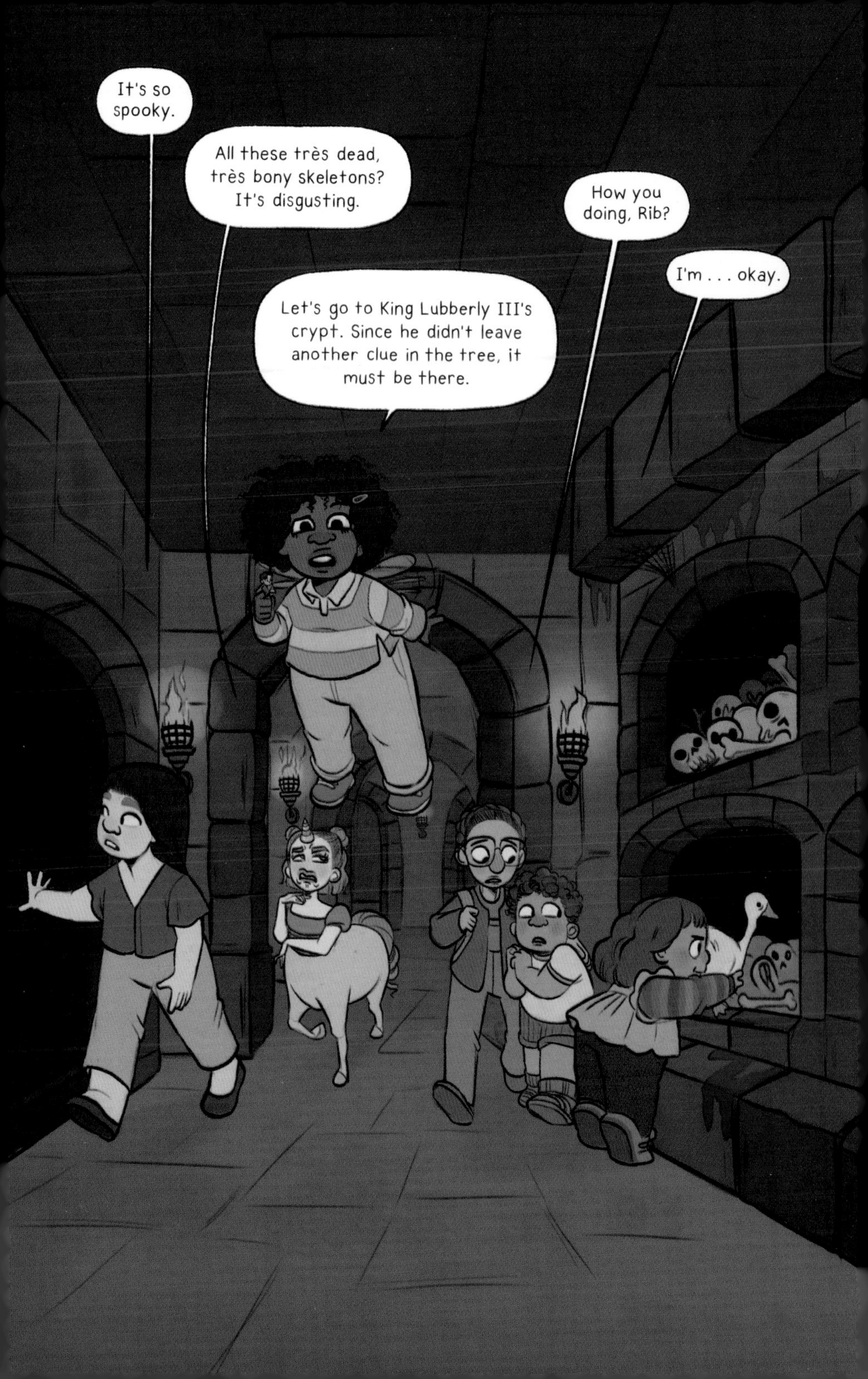
It's so spooky.
All these très dead, très bony skeletons? It's disgusting.
Let's go to King Lubberly III's crypt. Since he didn't leave another clue in the tree, it must be there.
How you doing, Rib?
I'm . . . okay.

We walked past bones and bones and bones till we got to the more royal-looking part. There were coffins with jewels and gold and everything.

King Lubberly I . . .

King Lubberly II . . .

There we go! King Lubberly III!

It was a huge, dusty wooden coffin with all these swirls carved in it.

A-are you gonna open it?

Yeah . . . yeah . . . just give me a second to work myself up to it.

Ugh, you big babies! I'll do it.

Voila planted both hands on the rim of the coffin and lifted it up. An enormous cloud of dust spilled out. And when we all stopped coughing . . .

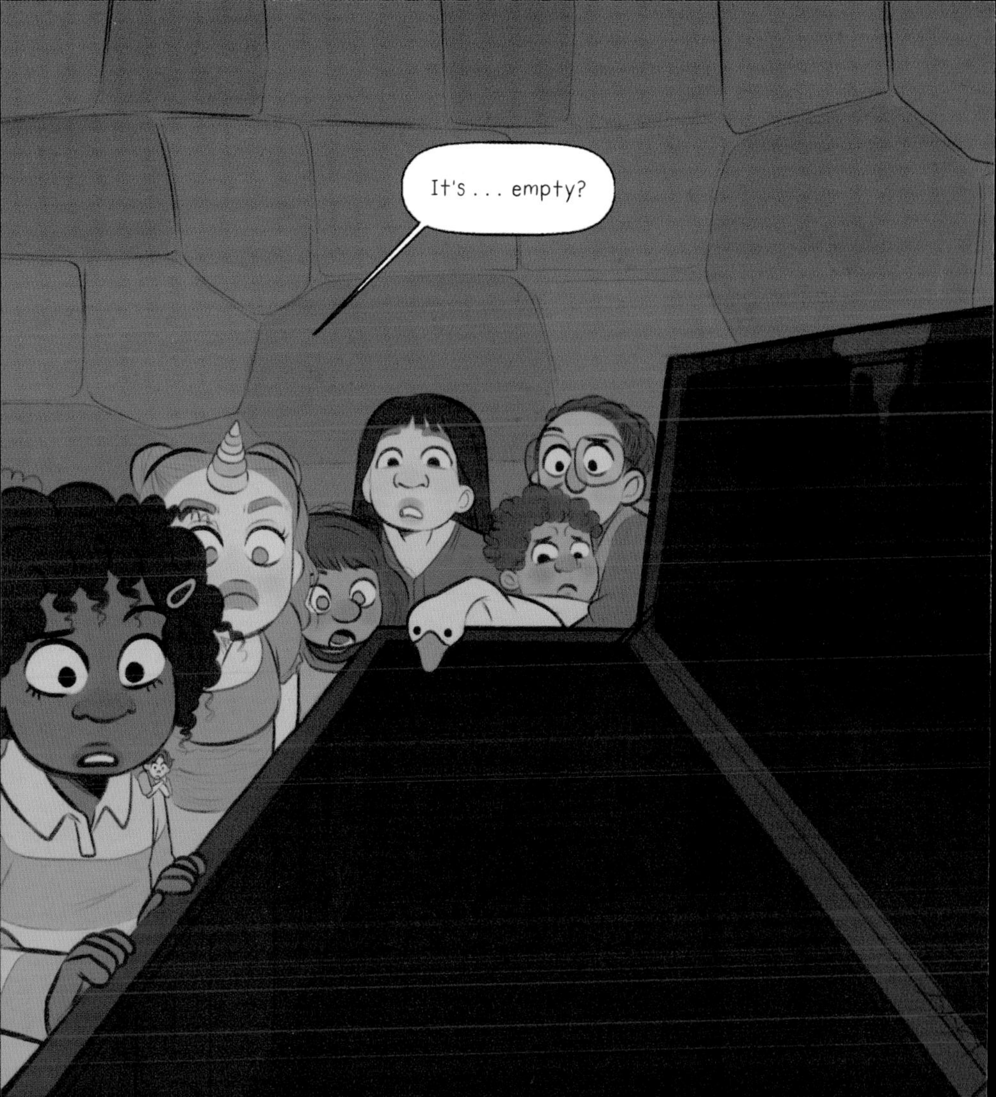
It's . . . empty?

We started looking at the plain, nonroyal vaults.

We all ran over to Schmitty. She was standing at the foot of this thick, wooden vault door. It was sealed with all kinds of locks and fastenings.

Schmitty jiggled the doorknob, and it made a clunking noise.
A hatch opened in the middle of the door.
A shelf popped out at us,
and there was a little wooden
diorama of Gumbling.

It had an inscription on it:

"On this Gumbling (not to scale)
Play me every Gumbling tale."

I was nervous. I didn't want to mess this up and let everyone down. My hands felt sweaty. But I had to think.

Whew. To do them in historical order, I'd have to start with "How Gumbling Came to Be." But how would I play that story on the diorama?

I had a weird idea, but I had to try it out.

I picked up Schmitty and sat her down on the model. Like the baby who shaped Gumbling Valley with her butt. Some parts shifted in the door, and one of the latches undid itself.

Hee hee! Hey!

Yes!

That worked?!

Okay, that worked. So I knew what to do next.

I pulled one of the stars hanging from a string down in the direction
of Starkeeper Star Farm for the story of the first Starkeepers.
Another latch opened. Yes!

I pushed a cluster of Hoofbeast figures into town for
"Pester, Who Bothered Hoofbeasts." A bolt popped out.

There was an eyeball near a figure of Feszhtmama. I rolled it,
and the eyeball fell into a divot and busted open another lock!

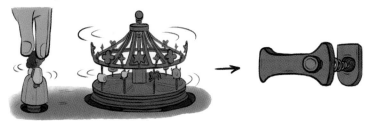

I twisted a figure of Princess Puzzline and made the carousel spin.
That corkscrewed another lock open! I didn't want to jinx it,
but I thought I was on a roll.

I lifted the pumpkin off the mouse's tail. A clasp unhooked itself.

I moved Maphew Garlic and the ghost along the river. Another clasp clicked open.

I spun Zhizhelle on the opera house stage. A lock thunked loose.

I switched the figures of Snowbilly Mim and Primbilly Mum. Clunk-thunk-clunk-thunk. Open.

And last, I lifted the figure of Lubberly III out of the castle. And the doorknob relaxed, like it had been gripping tight onto something and it just let go. And the door gently creaked open.

Way to go, Nell!
A-plus!
That's my sister!
No, she's MY sister!
That was so cool!
I'm slightly impressed.

I've got to hand it to Voila. She may be annoying and a total snob, but she sure can open a coffin.

There was actually a skeleton in this one. Rib squeezed me so tight, I almost fell over. And an envelope on a ribbon dropped down from the lid. I opened it up. Here's what it said.

Dear Reader,
If every clue is where I last put it, if it has remained in place, and if —in fact— Gumbling is somewhat like it once was, then I have led you here.

If some curious someone knew Gumbling well enough to follow each clue to this point, then that someone is you.

And to you I present the key to Gumbling. This key does not symbolize the possession of Gumbling. For Gumbling is not a land to be owned or ruled or turned over for her riches. The future of Gumbling ought to belong to those who remember her past, the good and the bad, and care for her citizens in the present. Thank you.

Sincerely,
Herdburt Blithely (formerly known as Lubberly III)

I felt around in the envelope and fished out a plain-looking, solid brass key. This was the key to Gumbling that was supposed to save the day? It felt like that part in that one movie where the guy has to pick which grail in a room full of fancy grails is the Holy Grail, and then it turns out to be the littlest, ugliest, most boring cup.

But this was it!

I held it up for everyone to see.

Then we heard a new voice:

The Greatman-Bigbys. What were they doing here?!

No way! The letter says this key belongs to people who really know and care about Gumbling. That's us. And I don't care what your family tree says—you're a bunch of phonies.

Yeah!

Honk!

You want to take away people's homes and replace them with a swim-up bar? That's the worst.

You don't care how anyone here feels.

You . . . butts!

And you have no taste.

They didn't look happy. Tom Greatman-Bigby pushed everyone to the side, walked right up to me, and grabbed my wrist. He squeezed it so hard, and I didn't mean to, but my fingers let go of the key. Then he walked back to his sister.

These are not very nice little children, Christina.

I agree, Tom. I'm not gonna miss them.

And then whoooOOosh-ka-THONK. They closed the vault and locked us in.

We'll come back for you after we get the castle!

If we remember! Byeeee!

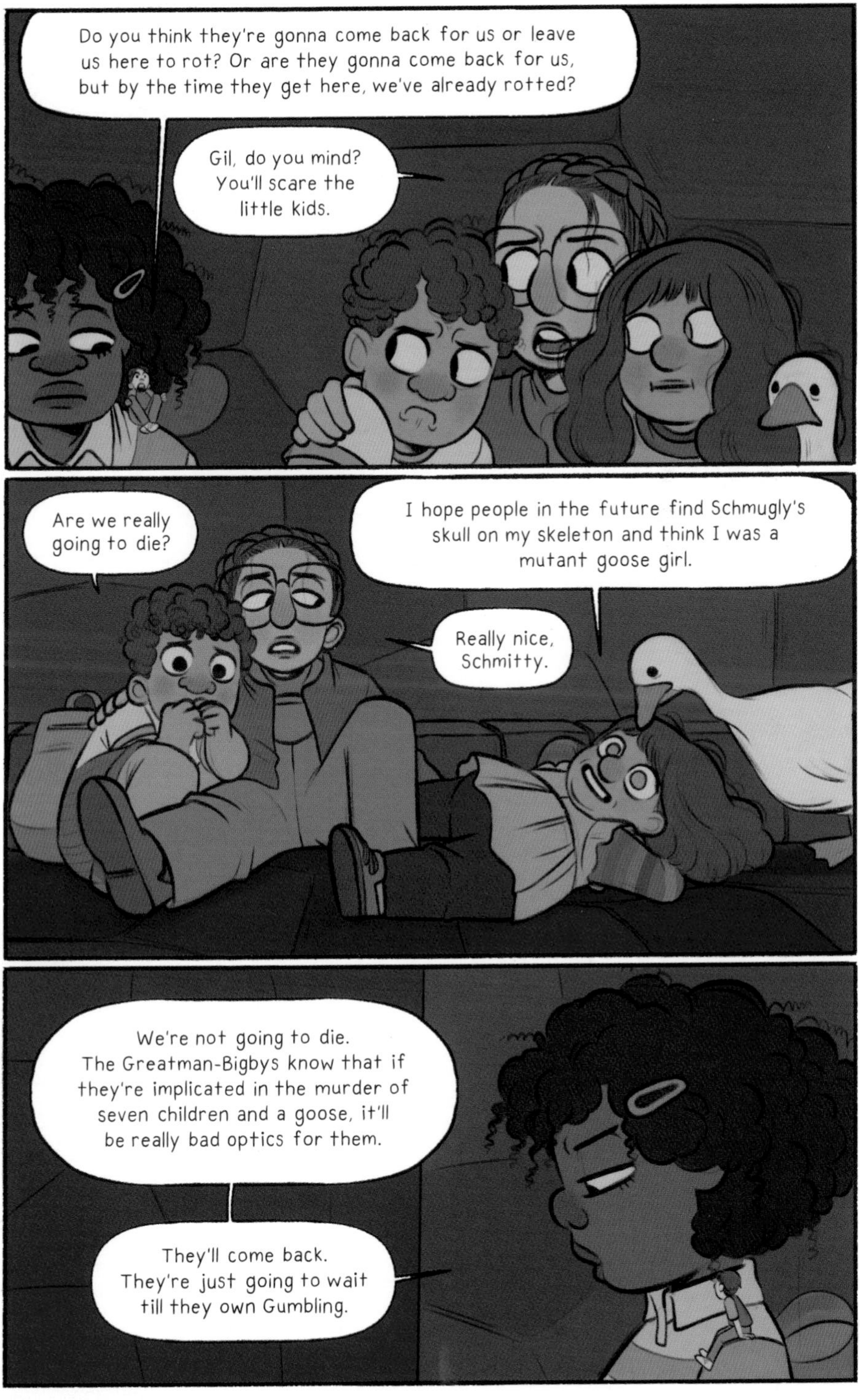
Do you think they're gonna come back for us or leave us here to rot? Or are they gonna come back for us, but by the time they get here, we've already rotted?
Gil, do you mind? You'll scare the little kids.
Are we really going to die?
I hope people in the future find Schmugly's skull on my skeleton and think I was a mutant goose girl.
Really nice, Schmitty.
We're not going to die. The Greatman-Bigbys know that if they're implicated in the murder of seven children and a goose, it'll be really bad optics for them.
They'll come back. They're just going to wait till they own Gumbling.

So . . . that's good.

No, V. It's not "good" that they're going to own Gumbling.

Um, wow. I meant good that we'll be alive. I don't care about Castleworld. It's whatever.

It's not whatever to me. They're going to kick people like me out of our homes.

Wait, what? Lee, I didn't know you lived in the castle.

We always hang out at your house. I never told you because I knew you wouldn't get it.

Of course I get it!

So you know exactly how it feels to have your life fall apart and have no control over it? You know how it feels to be so stressed about everything and even more stressed that someone's going to see how stressed you are?

You know how THAT feels, V?

. . .

Okay, well I'm obviously sorry. See? Sorry sorry sorry.

I guess you're as sorry as you know how to be right now.

Exactly! You get it!

I jumped up to touch the ceiling, to see if there was a hatch to pull down. I felt the ground for a trapdoor.

I felt so bad. We were trapped and it was all my fault. I got us on this hunt in the first place. I brought us down here, and I lost the key. I wouldn't be surprised if they all hated my guts. Everyone looked so miserable.

Well, at least I could help my little brother. I still had the charging star Pa gave me. Because I'm supposed to be the responsible one. Well, I guess I wasn't as responsible as he wanted me to be. I got everyone into so much trouble.

I just hoped the star could give us a little light and a little warmth. I pulled it out of my backpack. I had no idea how much it would help . . .

I spent forty-five years of my life ignoring most of Gumbling. I lived in my own private world and considered myself a god. I created puzzles and games that only I could really win, I hoarded my own private fortune. And I was never happy because I always wanted more. I spent the last thirty-five years of my life anonymous and very, very happy. I had less than I ever had as a king. But somehow, I had more.

How much time did this King Herdburt Lubberly Blithely the Whatever-th have? Wasn't he busy dying?

Wow . . .

Because I grew to recognize what was already here in Gumbling that made all of us very rich indeed. And that was enough. Sometimes we just need something illuminated for us to notice it's there.

One stone in the wall was entirely covered in the starlight ink.

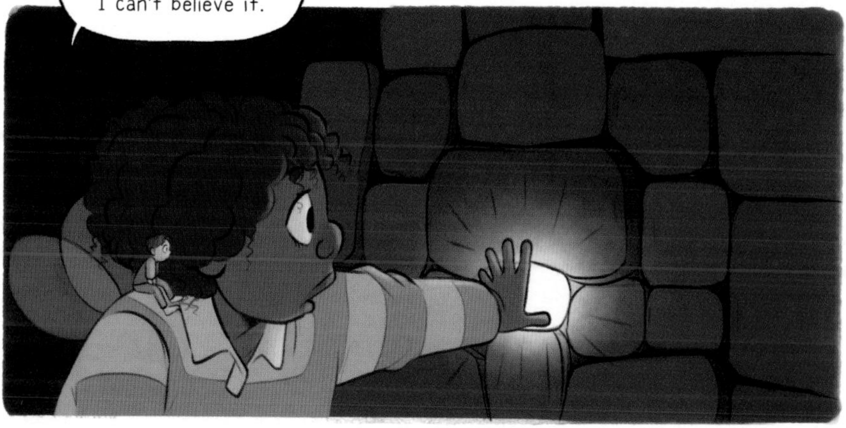
Oh my— Nell, you were right. I can't believe it.

Myra pushed on it, and a panel in the wall opened up, revealing a staircase.

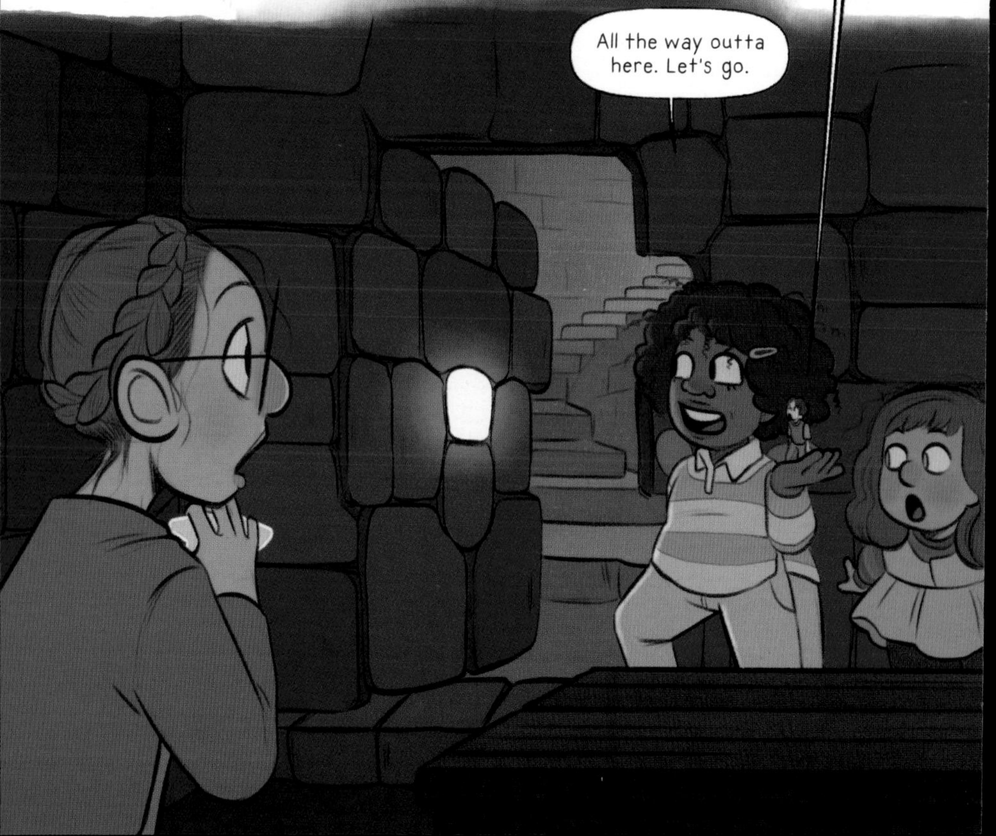
Cool cool cool COOL COOL. SO COOL.
. . . So where does it go?
All the way outta here. Let's go.

Voila hadn't started climbing the stairs yet.

Are you okay?

I'm fine. It's fine. They're . . . just a little steeper than I'm used to.

Leabelle and I went down to help Voila.

Thanks . . .

I really am sorry. I would've been a lot better if I had known how much all this bothered you, Lee. You're a really good friend. And I want to be a better friend. I can be better. Besides, I am going to make these Castleworld worms sorry they ever came here.

Okay. If VOILA can reflect on her behavior and work toward being a better friend, I definitely can. I'm not going to let her beat me.

Hi.

Hey.

Good job, you know, with all this.

Thanks. I can't believe it worked, either.

I'm sorry I've been so clingy and insecure.

This whole time, I had all these big feelings about not being good enough and losing you. And I knew they didn't make sense. But I took them out on you. And then that actually made me lose you.

You didn't lose me. But I was acting like you did, wasn't I?

Maybe just thiiiiis much.

Yeah. Oops.

I'm so sorry, Nell. I get so stuck on doing things my way. I didn't have to blame you and shame you so much.

You were just trying to help, and I couldn't see it, but you actually were helping a lot. I should have let you in more from the beginning.

You should have your own life, too. It's not the end of the world if we have our own interests and our own space. We're not losing anything.

No. Never.

Turns out, I could've actually used your help a lot sooner, Miss Treasure-Hunting Crypto-Mystery Girl.

I'm just—sniff sniff—so—sniff—GOOD AT IT! Waaaaaahhhhh!

Haahhaaaaa, shut up.

We got to the top of the stairs, where there was a really narrow walkway. We were probably still underground, but we had no clue where. Then Gil started making all these sniffing noises.

... Orange peels ... apple cores ... fish bones ... that's garbage! Keep going this way!

We ran till we saw a little bit of light and came into a clearing. There was a garbage bin and a chute above it.

Wait ... we're in the castle! This is the trash from the community kitchen. Our neighbor makes roust with apples and oranges.

We can get through to the council meeting if we take some of my secret passages.

Secret passage through what? That little chute? Even if I could fit through there, I'm not crawling up a garbage slide. Not cute.

No, no, it's okay! I think I know another way.

Leabelle got us all to push the bin out from against the wall.
There was an entryway! We all went through. She was like a spy
or a superhero. She knew where to go, and it was all so easy for
her. The rest of us could barely keep up.

Until we got stuck behind a grate.

It's bolted on the other side! I can't knock it loose from this side!

This is the closest bathroom to the archives. If Birdneck is in the library, maybe we can make enough noise to get her attention.

Did someone say "noise"?

Schmugs, this one's on us.

And Schmitty and Schmugly started honking at the top of their lungs (or, in Schmugly's case, his lungs and his system of extra air sacs—thank you, goose report).

Through all the honking, we heard footsteps.

And Birdneck did come!

Heavens and double heavens, is that you, Nell? You couldn't have been a bit subtler?

Sorry! It's an emergency!

Then Yabulga came puttering in after.

That's Yabulga the Witch!

Eh?

Um . . . hello. I . . . love your work.

They jimmied the grate open, and we all climbed out.

We have to stop the Greatman-Bigbys!

And the floor is almost closed to public comment!

What does that mean?

It means we need to go NOW.

You should come—you're both highly regarded grown-up voices in the community. We have a way better chance of getting heard if you come.

Well, I suppose—

Let's go eat those bilge-brained parasites!

So we all went up the winding staircase to the main floor, back to the town hall. All ten of us crashed through the door and into the meeting.

Stop EVERYTHING!

We have GAME-CHANGING INFORMATION.

Everyone in the crowd stared at us.

Voila, darling? What is this?

Leabelle? What's going on?

Mom, we came to save the castle. We came to save everything. They're frauds!

Everyone looked back to the front of the room, where Tom and Christina Greatman-Bigby were sitting. They looked a little awkward for a second, but then they switched back to acting cool and unbothered.

I'm so sorry you feel that way, li'l girlboss. We want to empower you to make your voice heard, but here's the thing: we're the heirs to this kingdom. That's why our ancestor left his key to Gumbling to us.

As the only one here who was actually alive when that dratted fool Lubberly was here, I can assure you, he had no interest in leaving his kingdom to profiteering dunderheads like you. He was very proud of how much he had changed. He was extremely annoying about it.

Yeah! He left a whole treasure hunt to the key for people who actually care about Gumbling. We found it in the catacombs. The only reason they have it is because they stole it from us and locked us in the crypt.

The crowd gasped. I never realized it would feel so cool to say something and make people gasp.

Wow. I heard you guys liked making up fairy tales around here, but this is getting out of hand.

They're not just fairy tales. It's our history.

And it's not something you can just sell.

We don't care if they have Lubberly blood. They're not here for Gumbling. They're only here for themselves.

Well put, Myra.

Now, hold on, we have several proven successes. We're going to make this town very rich and very happy.

I wouldn't be happy.

Me neither.

I would throw a fit EVERY DAY. And trust me, you do NOT want that.

We don't need to change Gumbling so people will want to come here to spend money. Gumbling is special because of everyone who's already here, everyone who loves it just the way it is.

You know, you really ought to listen to these children.

They've worked very hard and taken great pains to be here.

I went through garbage.

I went through all the town's bylaws.

I went up and down stairs and into the sky. In new shoes.

I went inside the castle's guts.

I went down into the really dark, creepy underground bones place.

I ditched.

Trust us, we have been up and down and all around and inside Gumbling. We know it. We love it. That's why we got the key. Gumbling is for all of us. Please, please, please don't let them take it away.

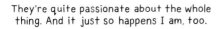

They're quite passionate about the whole thing. And it just so happens I am, too.

I never liked this whole stinking hotel business.

I'm with the kids!

So am I!

Listen to them. It's their home, too.

Tell these charlatans to leave Gumbling at once!

I agree.

Me too.

And me.

Fellow council members, you're all aware of my feelings on the subject. And I don't think anyone could put it better than these kids just did.

The council leaned in close to one another and whispered for a while. The rest of the room was totally quiet.

They make an excellent argument.

You so-called politicians are going to let a bunch of little brats push you around? That's how you do business around here?

It's really very unprofessional.

I should say it's more unprofessional, not to mention cruel, to trap children in an underground crypt so they won't interfere with your plans.

But hey, maybe that's just our uninformed, provincial politics.

I—I—I—

Get out of Gumbling.

Now, see, you can't just—

Gil just about died when Leabelle squoze his hand. He kept staring at his hand for the rest of the day.

The Didwells invited us to the Third Wish for celebratory Blowtorch Soup and ice cream.

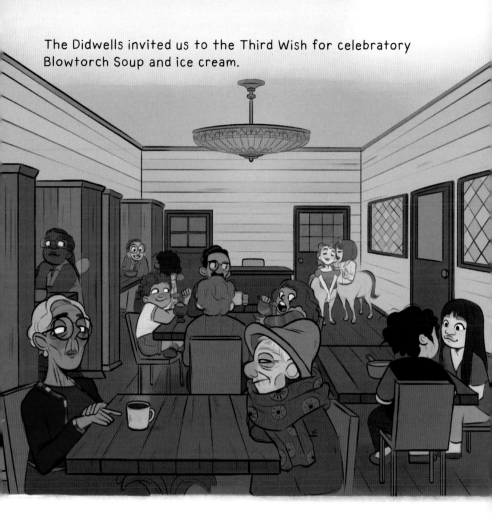

Sure, from someone else's point of view, we won our same-old, same-old town back. We're celebrating boring stuff like our right to keep eating mostly soup and fish and to keep using old computers at school.

But if you ask me and my friends, we learned how special Gumbling is this year. And we won back a town that we happen to really like. We're celebrating that we're already proud of where we come from. We're celebrating a community that takes care of one another and makes sure everyone has food and a place to live. It's not fancy or exciting. And maybe it's only magical and fairy tale-ish in a kind of dull way. But that works for us.

Dear Journal,

Today we gave our presentations on what we learned in our apprenticeships.

Everyone's families and mentors were there. My family got spots in the front row, and Dad brought his video camera. I kept looking out from backstage, and they'd holler and wave every time they saw me. Sometimes it's embarrassing to be loved a lot.

Gil went early, because his last name starts with a B. He talked about how Mr. Grubbisher's garbage wagon works, and he showed off some Thumbkin-size furniture he made out of upcycled stuff he found. I didn't know he was getting so creative with his job. Sometimes he really surprises me.

Then it was Myra's turn. She talked about the history of housing and public services in the castle since Lubberly III left. I guess she learned a ton in her deep dive into the town's laws. It turned out to be really useful. She said when she grows up, she wants to travel to other places and tell them about our policies. And it's Myra, so you know whatever future she's got planned is gonna happen.

For her presentation, Voila wrote a song called "I'm a Star, I Farm Stars." The lyrics were about star farming and turning stars into the energy that powers Gumbling. I couldn't help but roll my eyes a little. It was pretty hammy. But I didn't know she could write her own songs. And I never ever expected her to get into star farming. I looked out at Pa in the audience, bopping his head to the music and looking pretty proud.

Leabelle showed a bunch of slides of Wiz Bravo's process painting the opera house. She was really polite about how the apprenticeship had gone. She just handled the whole thing with a lot of grace, considering what a putz Wiz Bravo turned out to be. He didn't even show up to her presentation. But I noticed she just kept looking at her mom through the whole speech. It lit her up. Like Leabelle Oh needed to get any more radiant.

Then it was my turn.

I went up to the podium, and Ms. Garlic helped project my slides. And I began to talk . . .

I want to be honest. I thought I was really, really going to hate my apprenticeship. I wasn't interested in lorekeeping, and it didn't matter to me. I mean, I liked fairy tales when I was little, and it's sort of cool that they are our history. But I found it kind of hard to connect with the material. That changed for three reasons:

Reason #1: I got to know Mrs. Birdneck. She cares a lot about her work and wants to make sure people don't forget what makes Gumbling, well, Gumbling. We have different styles sometimes, but I don't think that's a bad thing anymore. Because she respects my style, and I think I like hers, too.

Reason #2: I got to bring my passion for art to lorekeeping. Mrs. Birdneck showed me some old illustrated histories of Gumbling, and it flipped a switch in me. I found where I could connect with lorekeeping, and that helped me find the fun in it.

I never even knew that, hundreds of years ago, there were people that were interested in illustrating these stories. And now I'm one of them.

Mrs. Birdneck doesn't even know this, but I turned some of the stories she showed me into my own comics. I was just going to keep them to myself, but then I thought it would be better to show them here.

Not because they're the best art in the world or anything, but I want people to see that our folklore and history mean something to me. Illustrating the tales makes me feel connected to them, connected to the people in the stories, and connected to everyone in Gumbling.

Reason #3: Lorekeeping ended up being way more useful than I expected. I had no idea that knowing these stories was going to help me and my friends solve a problem that we never thought we'd solve. But it turns out that everyone learned something these past few months. And our apprenticeships equipped us with knowledge and skills that helped us get to the bottom of something bigger than any of us.

It doesn't matter if we end up being lorekeepers or garbage collectors or star farmers or council members or artists. We'll always have this experience, and who knows how it'll help us in the future? I can't wait to see.

Thank you.

There was a little end-of-apprenticeships party outside the school after all the presentations. My family came up and gave me hugs and kisses. Schmitty made me a drawing (see below), and Rib made me some cookies (crumbs below).

Well done, Nell. You ought to be proud of yourself.

Really?

I didn't know you had been doing any . . . independent creative enterprises.

I'm sorry, I shouldn't have been making comics when I was there for work.

No, no. I should rephrase.

Yabulga came to the presentations with Birdneck. I formally introduced Rib to his favorite witch.

So that's what Ribbo's doing next. Schmitty's going to be playing with her bug friends a lot, since they all come out in the spring. And I'll be thirteen in a week, which means I'll finally be old enough to do the campout in the Enchanted Forest in the summer. All my friends are signed up. Myra, Gil. And my new friends, Leabelle and (yeah, I KNOW) Voila.

And I think I have an idea for what I want to do after that.

Birdneck! Wait up!

You needn't shout. Mercy, I can hear you just as well at a reasonable volume.

Even though my apprenticeship's over . . . do you think you might still need help in the archives?

She smiled the second Birdneck smile I'd ever seen.

I think I just might. But I don't think I can treat you like an amateur lorekeeper anymore. I'd like to start paying you for your work. And commission you for more of your artistic interpretations.

Really?

We can discuss it all with your fathers. I'd love to keep working with you. But homework and fun come first.

Fun?

Yes, Nell, I do actually value fun.

You have to admit, it's kind of funny.

She stifled some laughter. Then she couldn't keep it in. She laughed big, huge laughs, like heavy breaths after you run a lot.

HA! HA! HA!

I like Birdneck. I like lorekeeping. I like school. And Gumbling.

And my friends and family.

And drawing.

And animals and plants. And food and treats.

Maybe it's just one of those days, but I like everything. Maybe I'll wake up in a terrible mood tomorrow and hate everything.

But today I'm with everyone I like in a place I love, and it's almost my birthday.

Maybe something will be frustrating or annoying or painful later.

But right now I'm living happily ever after.

Nell Starkeeper
The Lorekeeper
Presents . . .

TALES FROM
GUMBLING

(in comic form)

The Soup Man's Wish

Once there was a soup-maker named Maphew Garlic, who brewed wonderful soups and delivered them in his little boat.

He traveled along the Gumbling River in the middle of the night, bringing soup to the sleepless and to those who worked by night.

He could see well in the dark, and he could balance when the water got choppy, for he learned to cook on a pirate ship in his youth.

One evening he floated past a lonely ghost, wailing in the swamp. Maphew served him a bowl of his favorite recipe: cream of pepper soup.

Will you take a bowl? Soup may not solve your problem, but I'd wager it'll help.

The ghost drank, and Maphew could see the soup run down his clear throat. In payment for his act of kindness, the ghost offered to grant Maphew a wish.

Any wish, eh? I'm afraid I can't think of anything to wish for.

I will stay with you until you think of something, then.

Many nights passed as the soup man and the ghost traveled up and down the river. And every night the ghost asked, "Do you know what to wish for?" and Maphew said:

Not yet. I'm sorry.

One night a terrible man-eating snake slithered out of the river and coiled itself around Maphew Garlic. He couldn't loose himself free!

As the snake coiled tighter and tighter, the ghost begged his new friend to wish the snake away. But Maphew refused.

Instead he asked the ghost to toss him his soup ladle and his oar.

And with his oar, he wedged the mighty snake off him. And with his ladle, he gently dipped the snake back into the river and shooed it away.

See? I have everything I could ever need in my boat! What could I possibly wish for?

But perhaps . . . ? I've got it! I wish to have a friend who would accompany me on my nightly trips. I wish you would stay with me.

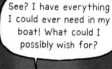

And the ghost granted his wish, and they lived happily ever after.

Pester, Who Bothered Hoofbeasts

He would pinch himself and cry out that it was his brother who pinched him. And he giggled to himself as he watched his scolding mother lift cake out of his brother's reach.

He would throw his voice and hurl insults to trick grown men drinking beer in the pub and watch gleefully as their fistfights poured into the street.

Ow! Mama!

Poor little Pester! Shame on you, Pintrick!

I kissed your sister!

You WHAT?!

I didn't say anything!

Pester Wamboom was a rough and warlike little boy who loved to start fights but did not love to get in trouble. He only loved watching others get in trouble.

One day Pester skipped by a herd of wild Hoofbeasts grazing in the meadow. He thought it would be funny if he could start a stampede.

So he pulled their tails and pinched their sides. But the gentle and peaceful Hoofbeasts did not respond.

Yabulga the Witch, who happened to be passing the meadow, shook her head.

That boy ought to be gentle and peaceful. Like a Hoofbeast.

This made Pester so mad that he began to stomp his feet and holler.

So, Yabulga being Yabulga, she poked her belly and twitched her ears and turned Pester into a Hoofbeast.

This made Pester so mad that he began to stomp his feet and holler. He charged all around the meadow, frightening the other Hoofbeasts.

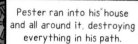

They stampeded after him, all the way into town. They crushed and smushed and left the marketplace a mess.

Pester ran into his house and all around it, destroying everything in his path.

Only, when his family came home, his mother screamed at the terrible mess.

It was a wild Hoofbeast!

I don't see any Hoofbeast here. Only a wild Pester!

Finally, when he had tired himself out, he sat in his kitchen and took three heavy breaths. This broke the spell and turned Pester back into a little boy.

So he received no cake that night. And that is how Pester finally learned not to pick fights.

Snowbilly Mim And Primbilly Mum

Everyone remarked how strange and wonderful it was. And as each year passed, the girls only looked more and more alike.

Once there was a miracle in Gumbling, when two identical baby girls were born to different families, the Mims and the Mums.

As soon as they could walk and talk, they became the best of friends. They loved doing all the same things: skipping rocks on the river, eating hot gumblebuns, picking flowers in the meadow.

But most of all, they loved to switch places and play tricks.

Snowbilly liked her own house, but she liked going to the Mum house and pretending to be Primbilly even more. And Primbilly loved being Snowbilly.

Every little difference made the girls miserable.

We're only special because we're exactly the same!

If we get any more different, we'll be two entirely different people!

But as they grew up, they started to notice little differences here and there. A freckle here on Snowbilly. A scar there on Primbilly. Snowbilly's left leg grew faster than the right. Primbilly's smile grew just a little bit wider than Snowbilly's.

So Snowbilly and Primbilly went to see Yabulga.

We want to stay the same! We want to be totally alike!

Please make the changing stop!

Please, girls. It's so undignified to beg. I'll make you the same, if that's what you really want.

It is! It is!

Very well. Go and bring me that mirror.

Yabulga slapped her throat and snapped her fingers and poof! She turned Primbilly Mum into Snowbilly Mim's reflection!

The girls laughed and cheered. Snowbilly twirled around, and Primbilly, of course, did the same.

But moments passed, and the thrill of being the very same was gone. And they both began to cry.

So Yabulga slapped her fingers and snapped her throat and reversed the spell.

There. Now I hope you see that change isn't so bad.

It isn't! It isn't!

And from that day on, they kept changing and growing, and they lived happily ever after.

Zhizhelle's Magic Shoes

Zhizhelle loved to dance. Her late mother taught her how to spin and glide.

Once there was a lovely girl named Zhizhelle. She was the only daughter of a wealthy Gumbling shoemaker, who loved his daughter very much.

Her father did not want Zhizhelle to be without a mother, so he married a cold woman with three daughters of her own.

They considered Zhizhelle a common enemy, which brought them closer together but was not very nice for Zhizhelle.

One day, before the shoemaker left for a shoemakers' convention three kingdoms over, he gave Zhizhelle a special pair of dancing shoes.

They're magic. When you dance, they'll take you anywhere you want to go.

When her father left, Zhizhelle felt very lonely, and her new family didn't exactly help. So she put on her shoes and danced.

Her father was right! The shoes were magic, and Zhizhelle was transported to the Gumbling Opera House, away from her tormentors. She danced and danced by herself to her heart's content. And when she was tired out, she magically returned home.

This, as one might imagine, became a regular practice for Zhizhelle.

They mocked. She danced. She left. They yelled. She danced. She left.

But one day Zhizhelle heard music as she danced in the empty opera house. She opened her eyes and saw a fellow playing the fiddle.

He was a sad young lad, in debt to his boss and worked to the bone. His only joy was his magic fiddle that brought him to the opera house the moment he started playing.

And so every day they met onstage at the same time. And he would play and she would dance. And every day they fell more and more in love.

People heard the lovely music and wandered into the opera house. And they stayed to watch Zhizhelle's beautiful dancing.

And the pair were so beloved, they were asked to be the main attraction at the opera house.

So they were free to return to the stage as much as they liked and dance and make music for the rest of their lives. And they lived happily ever after.

The Poor Little Mouse

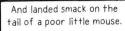

One day in the town square, a very large pumpkin rolled off a toppled pumpkin wagon . . .

And landed smack on the tail of a poor little mouse.

The poor little mouse squirmed and struggled, but it was no use. It couldn't move at all.

All the passersby in the square shook their heads and agreed:

Tsk tsk, that Poor Little Mouse is being crushed by that Very Large Pumpkin. It's just so sad.

More people gathered, and they pouted and sighed.

Tsk tsk, that Poor Little Mouse is being crushed by that Very Large Pumpkin. It's just so sad.

Until the whole kingdom of Gumbling had heard the news about the Poor Little Mouse and the Very Large Pumpkin.

Painters painted paintings of the heroic Poor Little Mouse, and troubadours sang ballads about the tragedy of the Poor Little Mouse.